Julian moved tow⋯ ⋯hat on a side table near one of the high, wing-backed chairs before the cold hearth as he went, opening his hand and turning it palm up as he drew nearer. "Veronica," he said softly.

"What?" she demanded, furious, pausing only momentarily in her tirade as she whirled to face him. When she saw how close he was, she clamped her mouth shut tight, taking a wary step back.

He smiled, loving the spark in her beautiful eyes, the daring in her brave but injured soul, and the lengths she would go to for a friend.

"I am sorry, that is what," he said simply. And then, reaching for her hand, he gently unclasped her fist and laid the package atop her palm. "Does this help lessen your anger in any way, Veronica?"

She blew out a small, ragged breath, seemingly struggling against a sudden urge to cry. "Drat you, Julian. You . . . you can be so unexpectedly tender at times. I—" She let forth another small breath, then said, "You continually surprise me."

"Do I? Pity that. What I *want* to do is please you, Veronica."

She blinked, amazed at his confession, confused by it, too. "Julian . . . you—you must cease speaking to me in such a—a familiar way, especially now that we are at Wrothram House. You—you are here as my guard. Do try to remember that."

"Aye," he whispered, tamping down the urge to gather her into his arms and hold her tight. "I shall try, my lady. But there may come a time, I hope, when you see me in a different light."

Books by Lindsay Randall

A DANGEROUS COURTSHIP
LADY LISSA'S LIAISON
MISS MEREDITH'S MARRIAGE
MISS MARCIE'S MISCHIEF
FORTUNE'S DESIRE
JADE TEMPTATION
DESIRE'S STORM

Published by Zebra Books

A DANGEROUS COURTSHIP

Lindsay Randall

Zebra Books
Kensington Publishing Corp.
http://www.zebrabooks.com

ZEBRA BOOKS are published by

Kensington Publishing Corp.
850 Third Avenue
New York, NY 10022

First Printing: April, 1999
10 9 8 7 6 5 4 3 2 1

Printed in the United States of America

For Melissa,
who opened her home and her heart,
and remains a true friend.

One

Julian Masters stood near the crumbling edges of a once-strong ledge, his black gaze centered on a beautiful female far below as she cautiously surveyed the vast and ghostly ruins he'd reluctantly come to call home.

He heard nothing as he watched the young lady pick a path, urging her mount closer to the unroofed and uncared-for abbey. He heard not the ever-present wind, not the sounds of the River Skell that emptied the wide valley spreading out in all directions around them, heard not even the sounds of his own breathing that grew faster with every pace she marked off.

But even though he could not hear, *he felt everything:* felt the lady's fear, the trepidation that clearly churned deep within her daring soul . . . and felt, most especially of all, her desperation.

Here, Julian thought to himself, *is a female on a mission.*

But for what and for why . . . and above all, *for whom?*

Julian's black gaze narrowed as he leaned slightly forward, having to stretch and straighten his muscular body to get a clearer view as the lady moved directly beneath him, guiding her mount to the very lip of an opened archway far below.

He noted the stylish cut and expensive fabric of her riding habit, the richly dyed plumes of the hat situated atop her inky locks, and he admired the lean, powerful haunches of the pricey horseflesh she sat atop so regally.

No milkmaid was this. No farmer's daughter or rector's ward, but a lady born and bred. Perhaps she was the daughter of a duke or a marquess. . . .

Whatever her blue-blooded lineage, she'd obviously been bold enough to steal away from any chaperon and had clearly chosen to invade Julian's domain.

His gut clenched at that latter thought and at the sight of the lady now sliding down off the saddle of her mare.

She clearly had no clue she was being watched, and just as obviously hoped she *wasn't* being watched. Her violet eyes scanning the area behind her, she looped the reins of her mount about an outcropping of ancient stonework, took a deep breath, then was lost to view as she entered beneath the archway.

Julian silently moved to the opposite side of the small expanse he stood atop just as the lady stepped carefully into the huge inner expanse of the abbey below. There was no ceiling above her, no doors or windowpanes—all had been carted away centuries ago, along with the riches this once-wealthy abbey had housed.

There was now just a lace of intricate, dove gray wall surrounding her, punctuated by more than a dozen massive pillars and huge arches cracked and crumbling with age.

She came to a standstill, sucking in a breath, those stunning violet eyes growing wide. By degrees, she forced herself to relax, to become accustomed to the vastness of the old abbey, and to the somber grayness of the walls that now held little more than weeds and memories and traces of the mist that would soon creep down in earnest from the heather heights of the far-flung moors.

Julian watched. He waited.

Was she friend or foe? Did her presence here signal danger . . . or was she merely some lovely sprite of the coming evening who'd lost her way?

Whatever or whoever she was, Julian thought her exquisite. Tall and reed slender, with midnight hair that could rival any night sky, she was beauty personified. The violet of her eyes matched the color of her superb riding habit, and her hands, encased in what looked to be the softest of kid, were finely shaped.

Julian let forth a long-held breath. It had been an age and longer since he'd espied such comeliness. The past ten months had been filled with little more than mere surviving and dealing with the oppressive silence that banged about in his mind.

This female's unexpected presence was like a burst of wondrous sound in his ears. Though her appearance at the abbey could doubtless pose a threat to him, it proved at the moment to be like a much-needed rain atop the barren desert his soul had become.

Julian wanted to dash down from the ledge he stood atop, wanted to enter into the area where she now stood.

Reason forbade such an action, of course. He had not stayed alive—albeit just a mere shell of the man he once was—for these many months by being careless. He needed to remain hidden and not make any rash decisions.

He backed away from the edge of the ledge, letting the slanting shadows of the setting sun swallow him, content for the moment to just watch the woman from his vantage point.

Her nervousness evident in the sweep of her gaze, in the quick, jerky turn of her head at something— some sound perhaps?—she once again took a steadying breath, then began a search of the abbey's ruins.

She navigated her way to the crumbling wall nearest her and meticulously examined every crook and crevice, getting down on bended knee to dig her gloved hands through the fallen masonry, then reaching high on tiptoe to do the same farther up the wall.

Not finding what she sought, she moved to the next section of the wall, and several minutes later to the next. Julian saw her frown when she came up empty-handed once again. Instead of the lady being deterred, however, her resolution seemed to increase tenfold. With determination, she continued her bottom-to-top search.

Julian wondered what she hoped to find in this desolate, forgotten place. He stamped down an urge to call out to her, to yell that there was naught but emptiness and memories within these luckless ruins.

But even if he dared to let himself be known to her, speaking aloud would be pointless. He hadn't spoken since that dreadful night August last when all he'd held dear had been taken from him in one swift, cruel act.

As he watched her, the setting sun turned the western sky a blaze of colors—from rose to lavender and then a dusky purple. The abbey walls reflected that breathtaking light, surrounding the lady in a rhapsody of shades.

Never, in all the weeks he'd been at Fountains, had Julian seen a sight so beautiful. It seemed this woman had brought the very light back into his world.

Julian watched as the lady turned her head to the

side again, pausing in her search, as though something more had startled her.

In the sky above, a lone bird that had been soaring and dipping instantly reeled away, doubtless cawing loudly as it flew.

Julian's black gaze narrowed.

Something was amiss.

Julian felt it just as surely as he had the lady's approach little more than a half hour ago when he'd been drawn by some unknown force up and out of the abbey's cellars and warren of prisons below. He'd climbed to the highest reaches of Fountains, where he'd hidden himself and watched her reluctant but brave approach.

He now stepped out of the shadows, his gaze hard on the surrounding area. *There* . . . in the distance, Julian discerned some motion beyond the walls.

In another moment, several dark figures came into view, pushing through the flowering meadows that sloped down from the moors.

Julian stiffened, his heart kicking in an uncomforting beat at the too-familiar sight of four enormous animals slinking forward.

Acting more like predatory wolves than dogs, the animals were wild, hungry beasts with matted fur and feral eyes. They were members of a pack he'd had to frighten off numerous times since he'd come to Fountains.

As one, they shot forward, their bodies low to the ground, their huge paws making fast work of clearing the distance between them and the unsuspecting female below.

Julian turned his gaze back to her. She'd resumed her search, obviously unaware of the animals that were closing in.

Didn't she realize what a reckless choice she'd made

in coming to the abbey, unescorted and unprotected? Was she merely foolish—or did her presence here indicate a grand and dangerous scheme on her part?

Unfortunately, Julian had not the time to dissect the situation, let alone consider fully the woman's motives.

If he did not move, and do so quickly, the lovely intruder would never have a chance to explain her presence. She would be dead in a matter of minutes.

Julian made his decision. Ignoring his own need to stay hidden, unmindful of the danger this curious lady might present—and forgetting his own predicament—he instantly moved into action.

Two

Lady Veronica Carstairs of London Town wished herself anywhere *but* the ruins of the deserted place called Fountains Abbey.

Situated just north of the River Skell, the sprawling complex of monestary buildings had risen in front of her like some ghostly specter filled with secrets. Forgotten for countless years, the mammoth place reeked of neglect and of a bygone greatness that now held only echoes of the past.

"Gracious, but 'tis a huge, forbidding place," Veronica said aloud to herself upon approaching, needing to hear the sound of something other than her horse's hooves, the wind, and her own maddening heartbeat.

She slowed her bay to a manageable pace, swallowing past the lump of uncertainty mounting in her throat.

Dare she go through with what she'd promised to her dear friend, Lady Pamela Beven? Dare she enter this deserted abbey and search for a package neither she nor Lady P knew more than just an inkling about?

Their plan had seemed so simple when concocted within the familiar confines of her family's London home.

"You *must* do this for me, Ronnie," the blue-eyed and very pretty Pamela had begged just a few days ago.

"I know without a doubt his lordship is not being as truthful with me as he should be." Pamela's pouty mouth had formed a frown in the face of Veronica's hesitation and obvious suspicions about Lord Rathbone's true character. "Now, do not go casting stones his way just yet," Pam had insisted, then added, "But it is my feeling that Lord Rathbone is caught up in something sinister . . . though this 'something' is not wholly of his own making, of that I am almost certain. I do believe there is someone plotting against him. And I do believe this—this *someone* will be sending a package to him . . . a packet that will be left at the Fountains Abbey in West Riding—or so my brother, Sidney, overheard at one of their clubs. Will you go to this abbey, Ronnie? Will you intercept this packet? And will you do so in the name of the Venus Society?"

'Twas a tall order, but Veronica found she could not decline the request. Pamela had become Veronica's closest friend in the year and a half since Veronica, with her sister, had moved from their family's country estate to live in London with their father, Earl Wrothram, so that Lily and then Veronica could be introduced to Society. Without Pamela, Lily's first Season would have been a disaster, Veronica knew.

Lily was now one-and-twenty, just a year older than Veronica, but she had the mind of someone far younger than that, which was the very reason her introduction to Polite Society had been held off for as long as possible. She was as naive as she was beautiful, and just as Veronica had feared, her sister had not acquired the Town bronze she needed to navigate her way through the sea of less-than-honorable gentlemen who sought to take advantage of her.

Lady P had taken Lily under her wing during that first Season since Veronica had yet to come out, and so there was nothing Veronica would not do for Pamela—even undertake a Venus Mission.

The history of the secret club known as the Venus Society was something not even Veronica could totally recount, even though she'd been its founder. The club had taken on a life of its own in the past year and a half, which amazed Veronica no small amount.

She'd formed the Venus Society as a way to help keep Lily out of the clutches of rakes who would lure Lily into their orbit with pretty phrases and empty promises. Every member of the club—and that number now totaled fifteen—took an oath to help aid the others in overseeing the gentle matters of their hearts. Sometimes, one of their members was called upon for a "mission," which usually involved the scouting out and, if need be, the thwarting of any plot laid by a possibly less-than-honest gentleman with whom one of their members had developed a *tendre*.

Veronica was certain it was because of the Venus Society that Lily's virtue was still intact. Her sister's breathtaking beauty, childlike innocence, and propensity to be reckless in her choices were a dangerous combination. Lily was continually falling in and out of love, casting her affections at men who were highly undeserving of such devotion. Though the Venus members had been effective in keeping Lily's virtue safe, they had not been able to stop the lovely Lily from giving her heart away again and again.

Veronica, unlike her sister, was not a female given to displays of great emotion. She'd learned at an early age to keep her feelings tightly reined, and she could still recall with alarming clarity the first time her father had raised his hand to her. She'd been but a child of four. As Veronica had grown older the earl's outbursts at her had grown in intensity. She had been vastly relieved when the earl took up permanent residence in their London home. Their parents' marriage had been one in name only, and Veronica did not wish for her sister or any of her Venus friends to ever have a marriage like the one her parents had shared. The Venus Society was her way of ensuring such a thing.

As for herself, Veronica had decided long ago that *she* would never marry.

Now, stepping inside the unroofed structure, Veronica wondered again if she dared to see this particular Venus Mission to its end.

"Just get the package and get out," Lady P had said. *Of course,* thought Veronica, *finding that dratted package within these lofty ruins will be another matter entirely.*

Veronica attempted to settle her nerves and tried to think like a person intent on hiding a packet within these walls.

She looked about her. *Where to begin?*

The place was a vast complex of pillars, bays, and weathered stone, much of it having been originally built on arches over the River Skell.

Veronica deduced she was standing now amid what must at one time have been the great hall. The space was enormous. Daunting, even.

How naive she'd been in thinking she could simply spirit off to Yorkshire, locate the abbey, then find the packet Pamela sought, as simple as that!

The abbey was monstrously huge, and everywhere Veronica looked she saw crumbled stone that could easily hold a package behind a well-placed rock.

Letting out a breath of frustration at her own lack of foresight, Veronica decided she'd best set to searching while there was still daylight to be had—and before her father's coachman, Shelton, who was little more than a jailor as far as Veronica was concerned, caught up to her.

Veronica began a diligent search, investigating from

bottom to top the wall nearest her, then the next section of wall.

Several times she was disturbed: first by the setting of the sun, which turned the massive walls about her into a brilliant display of colors; then by the ever-present wind, the nicker of her horse, even the cawing of a bird overhead. Heavens, but she was growing uncommonly nervous.

It would not do at all for her to allow her emotions to escalate into the boughs, Veronica knew. But though she tried to remain calm, the disturbing anxiousness she'd felt when first approaching the abbey began to ride her hard, fraying her usually strong nerves.

It was then that the first wild dog presented itself. Veronica's eyes widened as the animal landed its forepaws atop a tumbled fall of stones. The beast bared its fangs.

Veronica gasped, spun to the right, and was greeted by a similar sight through what had at one time been a window. Another dog, with gleaming eyes and dirty fur, clambered into view.

"Sweet mercy!" she gasped aloud.

Veronica felt instantly paralyzed, wave after wave of fear washing through her.

Of a sudden, two other dogs bounded into view, both of them hungry eyed and bony, their jaws slathered with wetness.

If she moved, Veronica knew she would be attacked and eaten alive. If she *didn't* move, the same fate would most likely befall her.

The beasts coolly slinked toward her with calculated strides. Like wolves, they seemed to have a master plan: surround and subdue her . . . then tear her apart, limb from limb.

Veronica thought to whistle for her mount, hoping

against hope the mare could snap free of its reined place, then charge inside and deflect the blows of the hungry, wild dogs while she heaved her body atop the saddle and attempted to get away.

But would the mare, so skittish on their journey to the ruins, be daring enough?

Hearing the hideous scratching and whinnying of her frightened bay, she chanced a glance toward the archway she'd entered into the abbey. The horse had caught the scent of the dogs and was now scraping its hooves atop the ground and snorting out breaths of fear. If the horse managed to get free of its post, it wouldn't come to her with a whistle or even a scream— it would simply speed away to safety!

Veronica jerked her gaze back toward the dogs.

They'd moved in during that short span of time— another few steps and they would *lunge* for her.

Veronica made a fast decision. With a strangled cry, she flung herself up toward an outcropping of stone, stretching and reaching as high as she could, her hat tumbling off her head as she did so. If she was fast enough and strong enough, perhaps she could pull herself up and out of the beasts' reach.

The moment her gloved hands latched around the stone she knew she'd miscalculated. She wasn't strong enough to haul her entire body up the face of the wall.

She smothered a scream, squeezing her eyes shut tight and trying to fling her legs to the side and upward. But her gloved fingers slid down the stone and she felt the snap of a wild dog too close to her heels.

It was then that strong hands latched about her wrists and hauled her upward.

Veronica, thrusting her head back and finally daring to open her eyes, looked up into the blackest gaze she'd ever seen, framed in a very masculine face carved with what could only be described as fierce determination.

Bearded, his black hair shoulder long and shagged, the man looked thoroughly lawless. He wore snug breeches that encased his muscular legs, sported dusty knee boots that appeared the worse for wear, and wore a linen shirt that had seen better days. His ungloved hands were callused but strong, and he seemed to have the strength and unerring drive of two men as he swept Veronica's lithe body up and clear from the jaws of certain death.

Before she could truly comprehend all that was happening, Veronica found herself settled firmly atop an outcropping of flat stone, standing flush with a man who had clearly lived apart from the civilized world for far too long.

Veronica's terror at being eaten alive was quickly replaced by danger of a different kind . . . of a more human element.

She swallowed hard.

"Th-thank you," Veronica managed to say. "If not for you, I—I fear I would be at the mercy of those . . . those animals."

But no matter how wild the dogs below were, her rescuer appeared far more agrarian and decidedly more dangerous. He also didn't appear to hear a word she'd said—or mayhap, he did not *care* to hear.

Whatever his predisposition, Veronica's rescuer pressed her back against the stonework, pinning her there with the full length of his body. She wondered if he was acting as shield between her and the dogs below, or if he had a more sinister thought in mind.

Veronica drew in a sharp breath, feeling the thud of his heart against her breasts.

The man's body was hard and firm, his arms contoured with muscle. He seemed to be an intense creation of nature—like a lightning storm tinged with thunder, or a hard rain fueled by a whipping wind.

He spoke no words, just held her fast against the stone, staring hard into her face. His intense silence frightened her. Veronica was just about to thrust away from him when one of the animals lunged upward.

In that instant, her rescuer proved no stranger to danger. He spun about just as the animal leaped up and onto the ledge. He met the beast chest to chest, then heaved it back down to the ground.

Things happened with a staccato pace after that. The man turned back toward her, captured her in a tight embrace, then thrust her to the left, out of harm's way just as she heard her coachman, Shelton, shout out. Immediately following came the sound of Shelton's trusty blunderbuss as the coachman, no doubt spying the animals, took aim and fired his gun.

A volley of sound reverberated within what was left of the abbey's walls. Veronica heard a screeching whinny from her horse, a growl from one of the animals below, and then heard her own boots scrape against stone as the stranger pulled her out of the line of fire . . . then plunged them both over the opposite side of the wall they stood upon.

Three

The two of them slid down a slope in the stonework, Veronica's body miraculously cushioned by that of her rescuer. She instinctively curled against him, hiding her face in his shirtfront.

Down, down they went until—with a thud that the man totally absorbed—they came to a stop within a small expanse of grass and flat stone. The area was flanked on one side by an outcropping of jagged rock that, thankfully, they had missed striking against by mere inches.

The world seemed suddenly to still.

Veronica, her body shockingly splayed atop her rescuer's, did not dare to move—not because she'd suffered any injury during their fall, but because she feared *he* might have been harmed in some way—or worse—snapped his neck due to how well he'd cushioned her.

Carefully, she lifted her head, her gaze skating over his handsome, bearded face.

His eyes were closed and he seemed frightfully still, all of which compounded the ripples of raw fear swirling through her.

"Sir?" she whispered. "Can—can you hear me?"

Nothing. No answer.

"*Sir?*"

At last he stirred.

"Aye," he finally said, his voice just a hoarse whisper, as though it had long been unused. "I hear you. Heaven and angels and all things blessed . . . *I hear you.*"

Veronica thought his reply peculiar, but hadn't a moment longer to think more on it than that, for he lifted his lashes, revealing fully his obsidian-eyed gaze.

At such close proximity the sight of those darkling eyes unsettled her. There was mystery in their deep depths, causing her once again to wonder at the danger he might represent. He lifted his right hand, startling Veronica further.

Primed by years of knowing the sting of her father's swift palm, Veronica reacted like an automaton, turning her face slightly to the side and steeling herself for the inevitable blow.

It never came.

"Ah . . . no," the man murmured. "I mean not to hurt you. Had you thought that?"

Veronica did not move or speak, though her eyes remained fastened on his.

"Ah," he said again, his gaze narrowing, " 'tis clear you thought just that."

He gave a click of his tongue and then, with a feathery touch, traced the pad of his thumb across her chin.

Veronica, unaccustomed to such gentleness, drew in a small, sharp breath.

"You've the look of a startled deer," he said. "Is it the memory of the dogs? Though the animals were frightful, you can rest easy, for they remain on the other side of the wall. You are not hurt, are you? No broken bones?"

Veronica shook her head, amazed at the calming effect the sound of his voice was having on her.

"Say something," he urged. "Assure me I am not

dreaming this moment . . . did not conjure your voice a moment ago."

"You—you are not dreaming, sir. Not by far."

As she spoke, the stranger closed his eyes, breathing in slowly and deeply. When he opened his eyes again there was a surprising hint of wetness glistening in them.

"Do you know," he whispered hoarsely, "your unexpected presence here has been both my hope and need answered?"

The man gently slid his callused hand to the back of her neck, beneath her curtain of hair, which come loose of its pins during their tumble. Then he quietly drew her mouth to his. He paused a second, as if to test whether or not she would slap him for his boldness.

She did not. Could not. And though he offered her every opportunity to pull away, Veronica found she could do no less than allow the moment to continue.

In the next instant, she felt the man's mouth connect with hers, the experience proving beyond anything she'd ever known or even thought to imagine.

He tasted of the blazing sunset she'd just witnessed and of what surely could only be described as desire. His lips were surprisingly soft, his close-cropped beard only slightly rough against her skin.

Veronica's eyes drifted half shut. Her cloud of dark hair cascaded down, curtaining their faces from the world and deepening the intimacy of their meeting mouths.

Veronica had not been kissed until now. She had never allowed any man to be so close to her as to take such a liberty.

But instead of feeling afraid or even violated, she felt curiously warm inside, as though the touch of his lips had lit a thousand Roman candles inside her.

Was *this* why Lily continually danced off into the darkest corners of London's ballrooms with rake after rake, no matter how shabbily they treated her afterward? Veronica wondered.

And could it be because of kisses like this that her dear friend Pamela was so willing to cast caution to the wind where the dubious Lord Rathbone was concerned?

That *must* be the sum of it all, Veronica deduced, amazed at the swirling of longing stirring to life in the deepest parts of her body.

The stranger, too, seemed overtaken by heated yearnings, for his kiss intensified and suddenly his tongue was doing the most pleasurable things at the bow of Veronica's lips. So much so that she longed to disappear into him, to be connected to him.

Her wish was granted in the next instant as he slid his tongue slowly into her mouth, tasting of her sweetness with a soft exploration.

A slight moan escaped Veronica before she could snatch it back. Oh, but she must be in shock—doubtless that was the reason for her lapse in sound judgment! What other explanation could there be?

Her reckless Venus Mission, the wild beasts, the fall, her coachman's gunfire—all had obviously succeeded in overwhelming her and numbing her good sense. Surely she was not sprawled atop some dangerous stranger, their hearts thudding one against the other, their lips melding together as intimately as though they were . . . were *lovers*.

The volleying of yet another report from Shelton's blunderbuss rent the air.

Not even a bucket of icy cold water tossed over her rescuer and her could have as effectively doused their flaring passions as precisely as the sound of that shot echoing about.

In one swift motion, the stranger rolled them both to the left, neatly tucking Veronica's body beneath his own and securing them under the shielding outlip of stone they'd been fortunate not to strike against as they'd slid down the slope.

There could be heard much commotion on the other side of the wall as her coachman, shouting to someone, gave instructions to fan out and begin a search of the abbey.

Veronica held perfectly still, fighting down a shiver of fear. What would happen when her father's fierce employee discovered his employer's daughter in a stranger's arms—and with her lips swollen from the man's recent kisses, no less!

Good Lord and good Lord, but the earl would bring the house down around her ears. He would strike her a blow unlike any she'd ever known in her youth.

Veronica's cheeks flamed. If the stranger even considered that he'd compromised her, he made no show of it. He seemed only at the moment to be concerned with the report of Shelton's gun and that her coachman was now searching the abbey in earnest.

"Damn," he muttered in frustration, clearly thinking aloud and not intending for her to hear. *"I have been found out."*

A new sensation of trepidation washed through Veronica. Gad, with what train of his had she involved herself?

"What—what do you mean you have been 'found out?' " Veronica dared to ask.

The stranger hitched himself up on his elbows. He stared down at her, his shadowed gaze revealing nothing.

"Of a sudden, it seems Fountains knows more traffic than even New Bond Street," he said, his tone deadly serious and his voice low. "Tell me, are they friends of yours?"

Veronica did not have a chance to reply, for Shelton called out her name. "My lady! Lady Veronica, can you hear me?"

Veronica's entire body jerked spasmodically at the booming voice of her father's most trusted henchman.

Her rescuer noted that reaction, and his black brows drew together in a frown. Suspicion clouding his features, he lowered his face to hers until his mouth was close to the shell of her left ear. "Tell me, *Lady Veronica*, did you lead your man here? Did you intend for him to find me, weapon loaded and at the ready?"

"*No.* Of course not!" she replied in a fast whisper. "How could I have? I—I did not expect to find anyone in this desolate place."

"But you did expect to find *something,*" he noted.

There was more commotion beyond the wall, saving Veronica from an explanation. Both she and her rescuer fell silent as they heard Shelton call out to his companion. "Drubbs, take your lamp and search the eastern end. She might have headed in that direction to escape the dogs. I know she was here, for that is her hat that's been trampled into the ground."

"Aye," came the reply, and then Shelton began calling for Veronica again.

She shuddered at how close the sound of his shouts were.

"Well?" her rescuer whispered.

"Well, what?" she whispered back.

"Are you not going to answer him?"

If the stranger had known anything about her life, he wouldn't ask such a thing. "And have him find me here, like this, with *you?*" Another shudder rippled through Veronica. "Heavens, no. Besides I—I have not yet accomplished what I set out to do here."

She scooched a little to the right, peering out just enough to see that the sun had fully set. Clear white moonlight began to flood the area.

"Blast," she whispered, knowing her search of the abbey was now totally ruined.

The light of Shelton's lamp could be seen through a crack in the masonry. He was standing directly across from them on the other side of the wall.

Her rescuer, believing Veronica to be vexed by the sight of Shelton's lamp and not the absence of daylight, motioned for her to be quiet.

Carefully, he lifted his body from hers, scooting out from beneath the lip of stone. He reached back, indicating for Veronica to take his hand.

Glancing once at Shelton's lamplight flickering in the cracks of stone, then at the dark-haired and clearly dangerous stranger, Veronica made her decision.

She took the man's hand.

Four

Making nary a sound, her rescuer led Veronica away from the spot where Shelton searched, guiding her round a bulk of stonework that cut them off completely from the pale yellow glow of her coachman's lamp. The rising moon illumined the area enough for Veronica to see a fall of tumbled rocks in front of and all around them.

"Now what?" she whispered.

"We go up," the stranger said. He tightened his large hand more firmly about hers, then reached out with his other to gain purchase on a jutting, jagged bit of rock above them. Getting a firm hold, he hauled himself upward, guiding Veronica along behind him.

Eventually, he gained the top of the huge pile.

"Take care, my lady, as some of these rocks are loose."

Even as he gave the warning, Veronica's right boot slipped on a tricky patch of stones. She began to slide downward, wincing at the sounds of rock shifting, then spilling down behind her.

"Blast," she muttered.

"I've got you," he whispered calmly, and indeed he did. In one smooth motion, he brought her up beside him, curling one strong arm about her waist when Veronica would have taken one step too many. "Careful," he breathed, motioning with a nod of his head to the area at her feet.

Veronica looked down, sucking in a breath. Below her was nothing but a black void of empty space. To their left rose one of Fountains' enormous walls. She hadn't realized they'd climbed so high, nor that he'd led them to the lip of a dangerous edge of stone.

"Oh," she gasped, instinctively curling her gloved fingers into the fabric of his worn shirt and holding on tightly. She turned her face to his, blinking at the sight of his dark visage now bathed in moonlight. Once again their bodies were chest to chest, and once again Veronica could feel the steady beat of his heart, the lean, corded muscle of him.

"Wh-what now, sir?" she managed to ask.

The look in his eyes was unreadable, for they were as black as the sky above them. "That all depends," he murmured.

"Depends? Depends on—on what, sir?" Veronica hated that the sound of his husky voice arrowed directly into the deepest, most feminine parts of her body—and devil take it but she was wondering if he was thinking to kiss her again . . . or more.

"Depends, my lady, on whether or not you wish to be led back to your horse or to remain longer within the walls of Fountains."

"Oh." Veronica felt her cheeks heat at where her thoughts had traveled. "Of—of course."

"Given that the party now in search of you will discover your presence once you return to your mount, and in view of the fact that you obviously came to Fountains for a reason, I take it you'll choose to linger longer within these ruins."

Veronica nodded, loosening her hold on his shirt and taking a careful step away from him. "Yes. Well. You are quite correct, sir. I am not yet ready to leave the abbey. Indeed, I had hoped to have a chance to—to look about the place, but—"

" 'Look about the place?' Come now, Lady Veronica. Don't you mean you wished to *search* it?"

Veronica frowned. "Yes, well, whatever. As I was saying, sir—" She paused as he pointed to their right, indicating for Veronica to head along the edge of rock. She did just that while she continued her explanation. "As I was saying, given the hour of my arrival in Ripon and my difficulty in finally reaching Fountains, I'd lost most of the day, and now . . . well . . . you know the rest of the story, sir."

"Do I? Hmmm. I wonder. But it is the beginning of this story that intrigues me at the moment." With alarming agility he navigated his way around and in front of Veronica. "Trust me when I say I intend to hear the full telling of it before this night is through, my lady."

Veronica swallowed, not liking the portentous note of his voice. "Sir?"

"This way, Lady Veronica."

With a familiarity that was unsettling, he took her hand once again in his, leading the way down a slope in the rocks.

"Now see here, sir," Veronica said, struggling over a difficult bit of slippery rock, but tugging her hand free of his nonetheless. "I suddenly do not like the tone of your voice. Though I am grateful for your aid thus far, I feel it gives you no license to demand full-blown explanations from me."

"No?" he inquired, allowing her her head and not reaching for her hand. He continued downward, letting her follow as she would.

"Absolutely not. In fact, sir, if you would but lead me to solid ground and the nearest opening in this pile of ruins, I will be quite all right," she said, with more bravado than she felt.

"Oh you will, will you?"

"Yes."

"Alone."

"Yes, alone."

"In the dark."

"It isn't *all* that dark," Veronica pointed out. "The moon is nearly fully risen and—"

"Which, by the bye," he cut in, a bit too chattily for Veronica's comfort, "will set the dogs to prowling. They've a nasty habit of that. Like to hunt by moonlight. Seem to have already taken a fancy to your scent, I might add."

Veronica frowned. He was now a good few feet farther down than she. "If this is your unsubtle way of trying to frighten me, sir, I'll have you know I am not a female given to hysterics."

"Aye, I've noticed."

"Nor am I a child."

He glanced back up at her. "I've noted that, too, Lady Veronica."

She decided to ignore that statement. She focused instead on the uneven stones beneath her. "I do believe climbing to the top was easier than getting down."

"This part of abbey is more ruinous than most," he said. "We're now coming closer to the river."

He was moving faster than Veronica. She found it difficult to keep up, for her boots kept slipping and sliding. "Drat," she muttered.

"Are you all right?"

"Yes, yes, fine. No, don't stop. It's just these boots of mine. *Blast.* I'd thought them suitable enough for my mission here, but then again I did not think to be navigating such treacherous falls of stones. Oh!" she gasped, losing her footing. She slid several feet before catching herself.

"Wait!" her rescuer ordered, growing impatient. "Don't move. I'll come back up and carry you down if I must."

"That will hardly be necessary," Veronica said, managing to retrieve her balance. "I am quite capable, sir, of getting my own self down from here."

But in her haste to hurry and get moving before he dared to carry her bodily down the slope, Veronica again felt her feet slide out from under her.

She wasn't able to catch herself this time. It seemed that every rock beneath her had merely been resting on the slope and was not anchored in any way.

Veronica went skating down, the skirts of her riding habit caught beneath her and baring the length of her legs.

One sharp, jagged bit of rock, though, proved solidly in place, scraping away some of the skin of her left leg as she slid alongside it.

Biting back a cry of pain, Veronica latched on to it, finally coming to a halt.

Her rescuer was instantly beside her, kneeling down. He had full view of her stockinged legs, the left stocking ripped and showing her pale ivory skin.

Veronica's face flamed with embarrassment. *"Drat,"* she muttered, thoroughly appalled at her predicament. She tugged her skirts out from beneath her, quickly trying to smooth them down.

"Drat, indeed," the stranger said, stilling her hands when she would have covered herself. His long, strong fingers skimmed gently down her thigh, stopping just at the point where the rock had left its mark. "You are bleeding, my lady."

" 'Tis n-nothing serious, I'm certain. I-I barely feel any pain."

The truth of the matter was, Veronica felt nothing but his hand atop her bared skin. Lord, but it was so large and strong *and warm.*

Her rescuer seemed not to notice the effect his touch had on her. He was inspecting her injury, his black brows drawing together in a frown she was coming to know all too well.

"It looks to be a nasty cut," he said, surveying the area of her thigh with a critical eye. "It is bleeding a good bit. You might even need a stitch or two to close it."

Veronica's lashes flew up as she turned her attention from his strong, tanned hand to his handsome face. "D-do you think so? Lord, I hope not. I haven't the time for such a bother."

"Well, my lady, it is a bother you have, and whether you like it or not, you'll have to take the time to tend to it. I'll lead you straight to your mount and accompany you back to—"

"Really, sir," Veronica cut in, aghast that he was suggesting she leave the ruins. "That is quite out of the question. I must needs have my look about Fountains. I cannot go back to the village just yet as I have to complete—"

"Bloody hell." It was he who cut in this time. And before Veronica could say or do anything to stop him, he brushed down her skirts, slid one arm beneath her knees, put the other firmly about her waist, then got to his feet holding her aloft in one sweeping movement.

"Sir," Veronica gasped. "I insist that you put me *down."*

"Insist all you like."

He navigated the last portions of the fall of stones like some ancient god of old thundering down from the very heights of Mt. Olympus.

"Really," Veronica said, having no choice but to wrap her arms about his neck lest she be banged about in his hold like a limp rag doll. "This is highly embarrassing. I am very capable of walking on my own."

"The devil you are."

They were on solid ground once again, but he did not set her down, nor did he slow his pace any. Veronica held on tighter as he effortlessly carried her across what she soon realized was an expanse of sheepnubbed grass adorned here and there with a thin tracery of fog. Moonlight bathed the area, making the sod look rich green in color.

She looked behind them, seeing the massive walls of Fountains jut high above. Somehow, the stranger had led her in a twisting path far away from Shelton . . . and somewhere amid those ruins were her coachman and a companion, doubtless still searching for her in earnest.

Veronica pressed down a shudder, her arms, seemingly of their own volition, curling even more snugly about her rescuer's neck.

He glanced at her, lifting one brow.

Veronica looked away quickly.

It occurred to her that she felt absurdly safe and protected in this stranger's arms. Though she'd met him barely an hour ago it seemed she'd known him far longer than that. Even the musky, masculine scent of him was becoming familiar.

She chanced a peek at him beneath her lashes. His gaze was straight ahead, because they'd left the grass behind and were approaching yet another piece of stonework. Veronica took the time to study his profile. The fierceness in his features that had at first alarmed her when he'd saved her from the wild dogs seemed now to have been washed away by the moon's glow.

His skin was deeply bronzed by the sun, proof that

he was a man who labored out of doors. And his hands, roughened and callused, though tender when he'd touched her, were further proof that this man obviously lived by the sweat of his brow and the strength of his back.

The one odd thing in the picture he presented was his perfect speech and cultured voice. It did not fit the puzzle of who he appeared to be. And in an age when fashionable men kept their faces cleanly shaven, this man sported a close-cropped beard—one, Veronica remembered all too clearly, had felt surprisingly wonderful against her soft skin.

Her quiet appraisal of him came to an end as they reached another stone structure of the abbey. This, too, was roofless and doorless, and it had long since been stripped of its windowpanes. It was more ruinous than some of the places of Fountains she had seen this night, but even so it seemed to be the stranger's destination.

He walked inside the structure, moving immediately to the right, where, Veronica noted, there was a cozy area with a small stone bench.

He set her down on that bench. Beside her, to the very farthest right, was a yawning archway cut into the earth. Cold air that smelled of dirt and, surprisingly, of the farflung moors high above flowed freely from it, indicating that it snaked beneath the ground to some other opening far away.

"Wh-where are we?" she asked.

"One of the abbey's many outerbuildings," he said. "The grass we just crossed over was probably a garden at one time, long ago. Doubtless it was watered from the River Skell." He indicated to her left.

Veronica turned her head, catching her breath at the sight that greeted her. She'd been so intent on the man that she'd barely noticed anything else—but, oh! what a sight she now beheld.

The opposite wall of the structure had long since fallen away, leaving in full open view the winding River Skell. The river now glistened a perfect silver hue beneath the moon's light, and it was skimmed here and there with feathery wisps of fog.

The arches and foundations of Fountains thrust up and out of her waters like majestic monuments of old, and the Skell, as though to keep hidden some of her ancient secrets, appeared to be a silver ribbon lacing tightly around their bases.

"Oh, my" Veronica whispered "It—it is beautiful. Stunning."

"Aye," he agreed.

"When I first saw this place, it never occurred to me that it could house anything so—so magical—so lovely as this."

"Aye," he agreed again.

Something in his tone caused Veronica to turn her gaze to him.

She was quite startled to find the man staring at her, transfixed—as though he'd been doing the very same the entire time she'd been talking about the water.

A deep heat suffused Veronica, one of a purely sensual nature.

If he noticed, he thankfully made no comment.

"If you'll wait here, my lady, I've something for that wound."

"Oh, y-yes . . . my injury." Veronica glanced down at her habit—anything but look at him!—and spied a deep stain of red on her skirts. "Yes, of course I'll wait, sir. But where—"

She felt a shift of movement and looked up without finishing her sentence.

He was already gone.

Veronica leaned forward on the bench, peering into the Stygian darkness of the earthen passageway he'd obviously just entered.

She frowned, then tamped down a shudder of trepidation. *Good Lord, what was he about?*

He returned a length of time later, carrying a lit lantern in one fist and a bottle of spirits and what looked to be bandages in the other. The glow of his lamp cast crazed shadows on what was left of the building's walls.

Veronica stiffened, easing back on the stone.

"Do not say you dwell in that cave, sir."

He shook his head.

"It is just a passageway, to another area of Fountains—her cellars and what were once prisons, to be exact."

Veronica relaxed somewhat.

He knelt before her, setting down the lamp, bottle and bandages. His eyes on a direct level with hers, and his face eerily lit from the lantern below, he said plainly, "It isn't the cave where I dwell, my lady, but the prisons. I find them very roomy."

Veronica forced down a gasp. "Surely you jest, sir. No one in their right mind would . . . what I mean to say is, why would anyone . . . *oh, blast.* Tell me, sir, are you a criminal or not?" she demanded.

"I assure you, I am no criminal."

"Are you on the run, then? Perhaps hiding from someone?"

Again, he answered in the negative, though this time not as swiftly or as surely as before.

"Earlier, when my coachman fired his gun, you—you thought that shot was for you, didn't you?" Veronica asked, deciding she might just as well plunge ahead. After all, she and this stranger had shared kisses and touches. What were a few personal questions compared to that? "You even said you'd been 'found out.' What did you mean by that, sir?"

"Exactly what I said. One can never be too careful these days, no matter where one dwells."

Veronica blew out a breath of agitation. "I vow, sir, you are being deliberately vague."

He arched one brow at her. "Am I? Forgive me." Even as he spoke, he lifted her left leg.

Veronica winced, not realizing how much her injury had pained her until now—as he forced her to straighten her leg out.

"Are you all right?" he asked.

Veronica nodded. "Yes, yes. I just . . . I am afraid to have a look at it, sir, for fear, as you said earlier, it—it may need a stitch. Or two." She prayed that wouldn't be the way of it.

"I have a lamp now. I'll be able to see the damage fully." With his left hand cradling her calf, he skimmed up the skirts of her habit with his right hand, pushing the material all the way up to and past her thigh.

Veronica squeezed her eyes shut tight. Good Lord and good Lord, but she must be a loose screw to allow the stranger to have such a sight of her uncovered leg.

"Well?" she murmured, thoroughly drowning in the throes of embarrassment and shame. "Is it terribly bad, sir?"

"Not as terrible as I had at first thought."

"It needs no stitch, then?"

"Not a one, my lady. 'Tis a nasty scrape, but not the gouge I'd feared."

Veronica opened her eyes. "Thank God."

"It will need to be cleaned though. And wrapped."

She looked down at him just in time to see him lift the bottle he'd brought. Brandy. A very old bottle, to boot. And what she'd thought to be a bundle of bandages weren't bandages at all, but a clean white shirt. His own, no doubt. And doubtless his only extra one, by the looks of his clothing.

He uncorked the bottle with strong white teeth and spat the cork down to the ground.

"Did—did you unearth that in the cellars of this abbey, sir?"

He shook his head, his lips tilting upward in a slight smile. "Until this night, my lady, I've found very little of worth within Fountains."

What a goose she was being, Veronica knew, but she thought his smile just then was the most handsome of things. And she found herself wondering how his face might look when wreathed in a full smile. On the heels of that came another thought—a puzzle, actually—of what he could have possibly meant by his words just now.

But in the next instant he motioned for her to take the bottle of brandy, and Veronica was brought out of her reverie.

"Though crass this might seem, perhaps a bit of this would fortify you for what is to come, my lady."

Veronica, her usual pragmatic self coming at last to the forefront, said, "Perhaps you are right, sir, crass or not."

She took the bottle he proffered, put the end of it to her lips, and tipped back a swallow.

The liquor burned all the way to the pit of her stomach, and though her eyes suddenly smarted, Veronica mentally applauded herself for not choking on the stuff.

She handed the bottle back to him. "Thank you," she said simply.

"Brace yourself, my lady," he advised.

Veronica did just that, curling her gloved fingers

about the lip of the stone bench, her body rigid and filled now with a healthy dose of brandy.

She took a deep breath, then nodded to the stranger.

Instantly she felt cool liquid splash against her thigh, then cascade in rivulets into her wound and beneath the rent in her stockings.

First came a raw burn, bone deep, one that seemed to radiate from her cut all the way through her body to her brain. It seemed that every nerve ending in her thigh was aflame and throbbing with each long, drawn-out beat of her heart.

And then . . . ah, then, Veronica miraculously felt nothing but the slow, steady caress of the stranger's open palm along the underside of her thigh. Up and down, and back and forth, slowly . . . gently . . . methodically. He could not have thought of a more effective way to take her mind off what he was doing, Veronica thought, than to stroke her thigh as he was doing now.

As he continued to massage her thigh, he poured more of the brandy into the cut. But Veronica felt none of the liquor's sting, only the warmth of the man's large hand, the touch of his fingers gently kneading the fleshy part of her thigh—higher . . . higher . . . nearly to her buttocks, but not quite—and then, swirling down once again, painting a path with his fingertips to the area just beneath her knee.

Veronica let out a breath, tipping her head back against the ruinous wall behind her, embarrassed at her predicament and yet not so embarrassed that she wanted him to stop his caresses. All she could see above her was the moon and the stars and the black sweep of night.

"Are you all right?" he inquired.

"Yes," she said. *No,* she thought.

"The wound is not bleeding as much now. Very little, in fact," he said.

"That is good news, sir." Good Lord and good Lord, did he not realize how he'd stirred her senses with his bold touch?

"I'll bind it as tightly as I dare. You'll have a physician tend to this on the morrow, yes?"

"Yes. Of course." But what about the rest of her? Veronica wondered. Could a doctor tend to all that this man had unleashed within her?

She heard the rent and tear of fabric, and then the feel of his hand was about her thigh once again as he gently dabbed at and around the scrape, pouring more of the brandy atop it. That done, he steadied her booted heel atop his own thigh as he used both hands to bind the wound with fresh strips of cloth.

Veronica, all the while, watched the play of starlight above, not really seeing the twinkling lights but seeing instead the remembered sight of the man's eyes and his half smile of a moment ago.

"Do you know," she whispered, head still tilted back, "I-I don't even know your name."

"You never asked."

She glanced down at him. "Well, I-I am asking now. Will you share it with me?"

There was a long pause, and then: "Aye. I will." He tied a knot in a strip of the fabric about her thigh. " 'Tis Julian, my lady," he said, his gaze on hers, watching, perhaps waiting to see what her reaction would be.

Julian. A name as refined as his voice, yet as unsuited to the look of him and the fact he dwelled in some ruinous prisons, obviously poverty-stricken.

"Just—just Julian? No last name, sir?"

"Just Julian."

Veronica let forth a small breath of sound, the

brandy in her belly and in her wound both warming and relaxing her, possibly even making her feel bold. "I hadn't expected you to actually share your full name with me, sir. Obviously you—"

"Julian" he cut in. "Call me Julian."

"As I was saying, sir . . . er Julian," she corrected, "you are obviously a man with secrets. I mean, you navigate the stones of Fountains as though you were born to them. You slip in and out of caves carved in the earth as though you'd made them yourself . . . and you—you clearly believed that my coachman's gun was pointed and fired only at you. Why is that? What are you hiding from? From *whom* are you hiding?"

It was the wrong thing to ask. Suddenly there was thunder on his brow. Finished dressing her wound, he lowered her booted heel from his knee, then got to his feet. He loomed over her, bracing his hands against the crumbling wall behind Veronica, lowering his face near to hers.

"You ask a lot of questions for someone who appears to have some train of her own in motion, my lady," he murmured softly. "Tell me, why is it *you* are here? Why do you hide from your hired man? And what is it you were seeking when I rescued you from the dogs?"

Veronica blanched. The storm in his eyes and the thrust of his questions were like a blast of icy air in her face. Suddenly, the effects of the brandy washed away and she felt fully the throbbing in her thigh. She was no longer certain she should have spoken so freely with this man. He appeared as he had when she'd first met him, when he'd lifted her up and away from the dogs—like danger on the hoof.

"Please," she whispered, "do—do not hover over me. I-I am suddenly feeling ill at ease."

"I don't doubt that. 'Tis a wild evening you've had.

I'd wager it's not every night that you allow a strange man to touch you, kiss you, as you've allowed me to do."

Heated shame suffused her. Rude of him to remind her. More appalling, however, was the fact that he was absolutely correct.

"Or am I wrong?" he went on, purposely goading her. "Do you, perhaps, simply have a penchant for quickly becoming familiar with *any* man you might encounter?"

Anger flared in Veronica. She shoved her skirts back into place and straightened on the bench—but the latter movement only served to align her face with his. The sight of his black gaze, so close to her own, was unsettling.

"Blast you," Veronica whispered. "How dare you speak to me like that and—and say such things!"

"Obviously, I dare a great deal. Now answer me. If I were any other man, my lady, would you have followed my lead away from your search party?"

"You'll not be getting any answers with insults, sir," she snapped, then narrowed her eyes. "Besides, I-I shouldn't trust you."

"No," he agreed, his tone growing dark, "you shouldn't, but you already have, and I'd like to know *why*. What brought you to Fountains, why are there men following you with weapons, and what *exactly* did the lot of you hope to find here?"

Veronica hesitated. Gad, but she hated feeling so cornered. What she hated more, though, was the thought of having her coachman find her without knowing a completion to her Venus Mission.

Veronica decided her best hope at retrieving the package was to give this stranger some half-truth concerning her mission. He obviously knew Fountains like the back of his hand, and he just as obviously was in dire straits—enough so, perhaps, that he might be willing to aid her, for a price.

"All right," Veronica finally said. "I'll tell you. I-I am here on a mission. A Venus Mission, to be exact."

"A what?"

"Never mind. It doesn't matter. What matters is that I find a certain packet . . . a-a package that was to be planted in this abbey at the height of Midsummer's Eve."

"Planted here by whom?"

"I-I don't know."

"And what is to be inside this package?"

Veronica frowned. "I-I don't know that either, unfortunately. All I know is that this package was to be placed here tonight, *somewhere* amid these ruins. And it is imperative that I find it. *This night.* And take it with me."

"I see," he said. "And what will you do with this package—once you locate it, that is."

"Deliver it to a friend," she answered.

"A *friend* who could not journey here with you this evening?"

Veronica frowned. If he knew Pamela, he would not have even bothered to ask such a question. The pretty Pamela was afraid of her own shadow, let alone striking out to search a place she'd never been.

"This person chooses to remain in Town, sir. Anonymous. It is their right, of course."

"Is it?" he asked, his tone indicating he did not agree. "I s'pose, so long as they've friends such as you, my lady, who will risk her safety for them so that they can choose such a course."

Of a sudden, the sound of Shelton's approach came to her ears. She could hear her coachman calling her name and, within a moment, could see the light of his lamp through the stonework. He was still a distance away, but clearly headed in their direction.

"Oh, my," Veronica gasped, " 'tis my coachman. He's found me." She quickly ducked under Julian's right arm and jumped to her feet, wincing as pain flared up from her left thigh.

"Found out . . . or *me?*" Julian demanded.

Veronica trembled at the dangerous look on Julian's face. "I-I know not what has driven you to live in some ruinous prisons, sir, but trust me when I say the man is searching for me alone. And . . . and do know I'd rather not have to face him."

"What the deuce has this man done to you that you are so eager to be away from him?"

"It—it is not my coachman who so totally frightens me, but the man who employs him. *Drat,*"she gasped, wincing again as she put the full of her weight on her leg.

Julian reached out to steady her. "I can lead you through the passageway," he said. "Can get you to the other side of the abbey long before your man finds you here."

"No," Veronica whispered, shaking her head, glancing out at the approaching signs of intrusion. "I-I have left him stewing long enough. I knew, eventually, I'd have to meet up with him. I should do so now."

"And your package?" he asked.

Oh, the package!

Veronica turned her face to his. "Listen to me, sir . . . er, Julian. It—it is quite obvious to me that you've landed yourself in dire straits, just as it is plain to me that you know every inch of Fountains. Clearly I cannot linger here through this Midsummer's Eve, though I'd like to. I-I am in need of help . . . and I am in a position to—to pay handsomely for that help."

"Go on. I'm listening."

Shelton's shouts drew nearer, as did the glow of his lamp.

Veronica decided to be blunt and to be quick about it. "If you will keep a keen watch tonight, if you will search every inch of this abbey, sir, I can reward you."

"Reward me."

Veronica nodded swiftly.

"And just exactly how, my lady, do you intend to 'reward' me?"

Veronica blinked. "A position, of course. You appear to be a man in need of employment and a solid roof over your head. Employment at one of my father's many estates is not out of the question. I could see you housed, and quite comfortably at that, in any number of shires throughout England. My father is a wealthy man. His holdings are vast. Name your desire, sir. Groundskeeper, gardener? Perhaps you prefer the stables? You could work for my father. I could arrange all of it."

"You go too far," he said, his tone laced with an underlying thread of some emotion she could not quite puzzle out and had no time at the moment to do so.

"Not all, I assure you. Nothing, no position, is out of the question—not if you aid me in my mission."

"It is that important to you?"

"Oh, yes. A dear friend needs that package."

Shelton, together with his companion, had now spied the lamp's glow. "Ho! There! A light!" Veronica heard Shelton cry. And then came the sounds of his feet pounding atop the ground.

"Good Lord," Veronica gasped, shuddering. By the sound of his voice, Shelton was in a furious mood.

"Just say the word, and I'll lead you away from him," Julian offered once again.

Another shudder tripped through Veronica, though this one had nothing to do with her fear of Shelton and everything to do with the man now standing in front of her, awaiting an answer.

For the briefest second she imagined what it might be like to go into the cave with this man, to spend a full night with him at Fountains, just the two of them, with the fog rolling down from the hills and the moonlight bathing them. . . .

"No," she said aloud, startled at where her mind had just now traveled. "I-I cannot. Just, please promise me you'll aid me in my mission. Promise me you'll watch for anyone coming here, for any signs of a package. I've a room at the Cock and Dove Inn. I can give you its direction—"

"I know of the inn," he said.

"So you'll do this?"

There was no more time for talk. Shelton and his companion were nearly upon them.

Julian had that suspicious look in his darkling eyes again, as though he believed all of this to be some grand scheme on her part. After a moment, though, he gave the barest nod of his head.

"Thank you," Veronica breathed.

He said nothing in reply. Taking up the bottle, the lamp, and what was left of his shirt, he looked one last time at Veronica, then slipped through the passageway and was gone, dousing the lamp's light as he went.

Veronica turned about just as Shelton and his follower burst into the ruins of the small outbuilding.

Five

A glowering Shelton—all six feet four inches and carrying a healthy weight on such a hulking frame—made no small matter of tromping into the small expanse where Veronica stood. A tiny, thin man—Drubbs, Shelton had called him—came skidding to a halt beside him, his eyes growing wide at the sight of Veronica standing in the shadows before the dark mouth of the earthen cave.

In one meaty fist, Shelton held his lantern aloft, glaring at Veronica with a baleful eye. "Good Gawd, m'lady, but you've scared the wits from me this night!"

Veronica forced herself not to tremble in the face of Shelton's baritone boom of a voice. "Hello, Shelton." She nodded to the small, gnomelike man who stood nervously at her coachman's side, dwarfed by his huge bulk. "Sir."

Shelton seemed momentarily at a loss given her composed greeting. And then, as if a mask fluttered over his bull-like features, he frowned mightily, demanding, "What the devil . . . what has happened this night, m'lady? You led me to believe you'd be with your maid. Then I return from my business to find you gone from the village. Alone. Unescorted."

Veronica flinched inwardly, but she refused to give any outward sign of how much this man intimidated her. He *was* an employee, after all. She tried very hard to forget the fact that he was her father's most trusted one.

"I-I had heard talk of these ruins and . . . and decided to explore them on my own. I was frightened earlier by some roving animals and—and hastened away. Indeed, I lost compass and . . . well . . . here I am."

"You did not hear my shouts?"

She shook her head, unable to say the white lie aloud.

He did not believe her, obviously. "So you are alone here, m'lady?" he demanded, not at all happy with her shenanigans and clearly wondering what was afoot.

So much for the man's true concern over her welfare, Veronica thought. Doubtless he was only considering his own hide and what would become of it once her father learned of the happenings in Yorkshire.

"Quite alone," Veronica answered.

"But I saw the light of a lantern." The accusation in Shelton's tone was unmistakable.

"Did you?" Veronica replied. "How odd. It—it must have been the play of moonlight, I imagine. As you can see, I have no lamp."

"Lawks, guv," piped the small, wiry man standing beside Shelton. "Inst'd of badger'n yer lady, ye shu'd be askin' whut spirits or demons she be seein' t'night! No doubt 'at be the light we spied." He made a quick sign of the cross over his chest, then pulled his threadbare coat closer about his bony frame as he settled his gray gaze upon Veronica. In a hushed whisper he asked, "Ye ain't be visit'd by *him*, have ye?"

"Who?" demanded Shelton, glaring at the man he'd chosen to guide him to the abbey and his lady. "What are you muttering about, Drubbs?"

"The ghost or demon that be hauntin' these ruins, that be whut!"

Shelton gave a grunt of disgust. "Do not be daft, man, and do not be telling such Canterbury tales in the lady's presence."

"No tall tale this, but the truth, I swears! Be it ghost or demon, there be sumthin' hauntin' the abbey. Seen it with me own eyes, I did, though only from afar. And I not be comin' near Fountains since." Voice dropping low, Drubbs added, "Beggin' yer pardon, guv, but it be yer coin whut led me here this night and not a thing less."

"And it will be my employer's blunt that will prompt you to lead us out of here," warned Shelton. "Now still that tongue of yours and keep your addled stories to yourself, else you'll be getting no coin whatsoever!"

To Veronica, Shelton said, "It is time to go, m'lady. You should be back at the inn. Indeed, you should never have come to Yorkshire at all. Your father will not be pleased knowing you came to such a place as Fountains Abbey, and with no chaperon. I am to watch over you until he returns from Bath, and do know I'd not intended to chase after you all the while."

Veronica's patience suddenly snapped. She'd spent too many years being watched over and dogged by her father's many employees.

But tonight—oh, tonight!—she'd felt unfettered freedom in the arms of a dangerous stranger. The memory of those moments were enough to make Veronica bold.

"My father," Veronica said in imperious tones, meaning to silence the coachman, "needs to know nothing of this evening's happenings. Is that clear, Shelton? Had I been but able, I would have come to Yorkshire without you. Though my father employs you, do remember that it is on *my* order you move when he is not present—which, at the moment, he is not."

Ignoring any reaction he might have to her words, Veronica turned her attention to the slight-framed Drubbs. "Tell me more about this . . . this specter," she said.

"What might ye be wantin' t' know, m'lady?"

"Everything, sir."

The tiny, gnomelike man drew up to the full of his slight height, his small-spaced eyes going wide. "Where ta begin?" he asked himself, and then, his face becoming animated, he said, "It all begun near nigh on a year ago. Fountains was deserted till then, I swears—nuthin' but the mist from the moors, some sheep, and the wild dogs . . . the same that be troublin' ye this night. Folks be sayin' the fiend, or ghost or whutev'r 'e be, fought off those dogs many a time—and wi' 'is bare hands t' boot!"

"Good Gawd," Shelton breathed, appalled at the guide's ridiculous story.

"That's enough, Shelton," Veronica said, very caught up in the man's words. She believed every bit of his story. Her rescuer had seemed to have little fear of the dogs, and he'd met the one atop the ledge with both steely nerve and unerring strength.

"Continue," Veronica urged the little man.

"He will *not,*" Shelton cut in.

Veronica cast the coachman a quelling look.

The small guide ignored Shelton's warning. To Veronica he said, "I will at 'at, but not in 'is place, w' 'at yawnin' black 'ole nearby. Beggin' yer pard'n, m'lady, but it be in the black, and out o' caves like 'at one, 'at the specter makes itself known."

"Very well then," said Veronica, eager to get her coachman and the guide away from where Julian had gone. "Let us head back to the main of the abbey. You can tell your story as we go."

Shelton, not at all pleased, had no choice but to do as his lady suggested. The three of them headed out of the ruinous building.

"So you have seen a man here?" Veronica asked Drubbs as they walked.

"If it *be* a man. Chock-full 'o madness, it wuz—all wild ey'd, 'air like Samson's own, beard un-trimmed . . ."

"I see," Veronica murmured. "And the man's name? His origins? Does anyone know?" she asked, refusing yet again to acknowledge Shelton's frown.

The guide shook his head. "No one knows. But 'e be called The Riv'rkeep by all who dwell in the shire."

"Riverkeep? Why is that?"

" 'E's said t' 'ave a path 'longside the riv'r, clearin' brush fer the animals and fer the trout in the wat'r. I sees 'im meself, walk'n the water's edge, keepin' close, as if the Riv'r Skell gives 'im power—but only in the darkest of night did I git such a glimpse, mind ye, and only a quick glimpse at 'at. There be others claim 'e walks the insides of Fount'ns and whut sees 'is black eyes lookin' out. Watchin' fer somethin' or *someone*."

"How interesting."

"It be said, too, m'lady 'at 'e be deaf as the day is long."

"Deaf?"

"Aye. Can't 'ear a thing. Could shout at 'im from afar and get no response, m'lady. But try t' get closer, and 'e senses yer presence right fast. The Riv'rkeep be said t' feel *all* things, m'lady. Ev'n be decipherin' a person's thoughts."

Veronica felt a tingle whirl up her spine at this last bit of news. Had Julian deciphered *her* thoughts while he'd been kissing her?

Veronica pushed the notion aside, not liking what the memory of his mouth on hers did to her heartbeat. She needed to keep her composure about her and not give Shelton any indication that she'd actually met this mysterious Riverkeep, let alone been touched and held by the man.

She turned her mind to the guide's description of Julian. Deaf, he'd said. That would explain Julian's words to her earlier and the moistness she'd seen in his eyes upon hearing her speak. Heavens, but their tumble and the blow he'd suffered during the fall must have had something to do with the restoration of his hearing. Doubtless hers had been the first voice he'd heard . . . but in how long? she wondered. Drubbs had mentioned something about twelve months. Could Julian have been at Fountains for such a length of time?

She shuddered inwardly, imagining Julian, alone and deaf, walking among these ruins month after month. What a beastly way to exist.

But what had forced him here? From what or whom had he fled? And why, of all places, had he chosen Fountains?

"Be 'e demon or ghost, m'lady," the guide continued, cutting into Veronica's thoughts, " 'e be trouble fer sure—eyes black as the very Pit, the soul within 'im just as fright fill'd, no doubt."

Veronica stumbled slightly over a step, but quickly righted herself. "Surely you don't believe that, sir. Why would you say such a thing?"

"Only the devil 'imself, a specter, or a man wi' an evil past would live such a life, I 'spect. If the Riv'rkeep be a man o' flesh-and-blood—which I doubt—then a dangerous sort 'e be."

This time, Veronica could not conceal the shudder that stole through her. Yes, Julian had appeared to be a man with something to hide. But was the cause of his hiding some fiendish act done *to* him, or *by* him?

Veronica's shiver deepened as she remembered suddenly that she'd given him her direction, had told him where she'd be spending the night. Had she made a dreadful mistake in sharing with the dangerous stranger what little she had about her Venus Mission?

Shelton, eyeing his lady, noted her sudden unease. Thoroughly disgusted by all this talk, he glowered at Drubbs and barked, "Enough talk, man. Just lead the way out of this gawdforsaken place."

Veronica sent a glance at her coachman, but decided not to object further. Shelton was as good as the right hand of her father. He'd been handpicked by Earl Wrothram to act as coachman to his daughters, not because Shelton harbored any skills greater than other coachmen, but simply because he could be trusted to carry out her father's exact word.

Ever versatile, and working his way up through various positions within the nobility, Shelton clearly knew on which side his bread was buttered. He had been many things during his life of serving the titled swells of Polite Society—a veritable henchman long ago for a vicious old crone of a lord full of thunder and vengeance, after that an instructor of boxing for the gentlemen in Town who liked such a sport . . . and for the past ten years, coachman to Veronica's family, his every move overseen by Earl Wrothram.

Shelton's allegiance to the earl was great, and his allegiance was further assured by the hefty coin he earned for dogging the steps of his employer's youngest daughter.

For some reason Veronica had yet to puzzle out, her father seemed to think she would one day make a mockery of him. Though it was the sweet, too-beautiful Lily whom the members of the Venus

Society were continually saving from certain scandal due to her penchant for falling in love with every man who cast an empty compliment her way, it was Veronica whom the earl seemed not to trust. Veronica could go nowhere but that the coachman knew of it, and she could do nothing but that Shelton eventually got wind of it.

That Veronica had managed to outsmart Shelton and get to Fountains Abbey long before he'd arrived was nothing short of miraculous.

Now that he'd found her, though, Veronica knew she'd have to be twice as conniving to get out from under his watchful eye ever again.

Veronica allowed Shelton his tiny victory of manipulating the moment, but only because she'd heard enough from the gnomelike Drubbs.

Despite what the locals thought about The Riverkeep—and despite the fact Veronica could only imagine about Julian's nefarious past or lack thereof—she had to believe in her conclusion that he was the very person, *the only person,* who could help see this particular Venus Mission to a successful conclusion.

It was with that thought in mind that Veronica willingly allowed the guide and Shelton to lead her back to the horses, and then far away from the ruins of Fountains.

She glanced back only once.

The sight she saw took her breath away. The pale radiance of the moon cast the jutting stones of the abbey into a place of wonder and mystery.

Was Julian watching their retreat?

Odd, but Veronica felt certain that he was.

Felt, too, that she was not the same person she'd been when she'd first come upon the ancient abbey and her dangerous rescuer.

Veronica swallowed, then turned her face back to
the road in front of her.

A long Midsummer's Eve night lay ahead.

High up on a massive wall stood Julian, one dusty
boot propped on a bit of stone, his right elbow anchored on his knee and his right hand stroking his
bearded chin. He was positioned at an opening that
had once been a window, beneath an arch of what had
at one time been delicately wrought stone lace.

From his vantage point he watched as the speck of
light that was the sum of the trio's lanterns grew dimmer and dimmer as the three made haste from the
abbey's sprawling lands.

He had waited in the earthen cavern, his lamp ex-
tinguished. He'd not fully believed the lady's wild
story of having to come to Fountains in search of a
packet, and he had wondered if she would send the
coachman and his companion into the cave after him.

But there had been no ambush in the passageway,
and so Julian had decided there must be some truth
in the lady's tale. Given that, and the fact she appeared
so terrified of her servant, he'd waited until he was
assured Lady Veronica would not be abused in anyway
by the gun-toting coachman.

She'd held her ground well in the face of her coachman's questions. As for the other man . . . well, Julian
had not been pleased to hear that he was thought to
be a specter, a demon even. What rubbish.

And yet . . . the tale the man had told was not so far
off the mark. Julian *had* felt like a specter when he'd
first arrived at the ruinous abbey, his hearing gone,
his heart torn asunder. And for ten long months he
had done naught but hide from the light of day in the
heart of Fountains's ancient prisons.

But tonight he'd met Veronica and heard her speak. The sound of her voice in his ears had reawakened his world-weary soul, and the feel and taste of her had brought to life in him a hunger he'd not known in a long, long while.

After exiting the earthen cavern once Veronica and her followers had gone, Julian had climbed to the highest ledge of Fountains, letting the wind tear at his long hair, allowing the wondrous sounds of night to pour over and through him. And he'd known in that instant that he was not the dead shell of a man he'd been when he saved Veronica from the wild dogs.

He now felt renewed purpose and knew a kernel of hope.

Whether by divinity, accident or supreme plotting, the violet-eyed Veronica had proved to be a catalyst, yanking him out of a dreary place he'd been for far too long.

What exactly her presence at Fountains this night meant, though, not even Julian could guess. For good or ill, it was a mystery he intended to unravel.

Veronica was silent during the long ride back to the inn. She did not allow her coachman's accusatory mood to force her into any explanation of her wanderings. The man was an employee, she reminded herself. He did not need to know what she was about, or even the why of it.

They soon reached the village.

While Fountains had been an oasis filled with moonlight and mist once the dogs had gone, the village presented an altogether different atmosphere. Several bonfires had been lit in celebration of Midsummer's Eve, and everywhere Veronica looked there were people milling and moving about, their laughing faces wreathed in the fires' light. It seemed a mad celebration had begun—one likely not to end until dawn. The magic of summer had descended; the merriment was loud and raucous.

Veronica's only thought was that she'd not stayed at Fountains long. Perhaps the person intending to deposit Rathbone's packet was among these revelers. Perhaps that person was getting a bellyful of food and drink and would strike out much later for the abbey.

As soon as they reached the inn, Veronica slid down off her saddle, leaving Shelton to oversee the managing of the cattle for the night. Then she scurried inside, moving quickly up the steps to her rented room. She could hear the shouts of voices outside, could see the light of the bonfires flickering through the thin-paned glass window on the first landing.

Finally reaching her room, Veronica thrust the door open.

Her maid jumped to her feet at the sight of her.

"La, m'lady," said the brown-haired, brown-eyed Nettie, "I feared you'd met a foul end this night, and yer coachman, well, he near box'd me ears fer losin' sight of you! Oh, please, I beg, d'not be runnin' away like that ag'n, m'lady—beggin' yer pardon I be fer ev'n sayin' such words!"

With a calm voice that belied the inner turmoil she was feeling, Veronica said, "You need not worry about anything, Nettie. I've returned now and am no more the worse for wear, I assure you."

"Awwks, m'lady, are you certain sure?"

"Yes. Very."

"But yer clothes be that rumpled, yer hat clean gone. Yer 'air, it be come undone frum its many pins . . . and—and yer *eyes*, m'lady!"

"What *about* my eyes, Nettie?"

The maid shrank back. "Nuthin'," she muttered

and then, unable to help herself, and with a grimace for fear she'd be reprimanded, added nonetheless, "Other than m'lady be lookin' as though she just met 'er death . . . or ma'hap the light of 'er life."

Veronica blinked. "Do not be absurd, Nettie." But even as Veronica said the words, she wondered if the transformation in her soul was so very evident that her flighty maid should notice. Veronica fought for some semblance of emotion. "I've encountered neither, Nettie. Now, if it would not be too much trouble, I'd like hot water for a bath."

"Yes, m'lady. It be no trouble, o' course."

"And I'm famished, Nettie. Please see that a private parlour is prepared downstairs."

"Yes, m'lady." The girl seemed eager to be gone.

"And, Nettie?"

"Yes?" she asked, poised by the door like a nervous bird ready to spring from a cage.

"I—I seemed to have scraped my leg during my expedition this evening. Could you perhaps ask below-stairs for any antiseptic that might be available?"

Nettie's brown eyes widened, but she wisely bit back any questions she might have of her lady's wanderings.

"Yes, m'lady. O' course."

The abigail nodded nervously, sketched what she clearly hoped was a proper curtsy, then hurried out of the room, leaving Veronica alone in the spacious bedchamber with its huge bed.

Veronica heaved a sigh of relief now that she had her servants busy with their business.

She glanced down at her skirts, wincing at the stain of blood near her left thigh. The cover of night had kept the sight from Shelton, no doubt. It had taken all of Veronica's strength not to limp back to her mount while at Fountains. She'd put up a brave front, not daring to let her coachman realize she'd been injured.

She now gently pressed her hand atop her left thigh, feeling fully the bandage Julian had wrapped about her scrape. He'd tied the strips of cloth tight, but not too tightly.

Veronica's cheeks warmed at the memory of his ministrations and the remembered feel of his callused but gentle hand along the underside of her thigh. Gad, but he'd near taken her breath away with the feel of his soft touch. And with his kisses, to boot, she thought, the heat in her face deepening.

Taking a deep, steadying breath, Veronica decided she'd best not dwell on what had transpired betwixt her and the dangerous stranger while at the abbey. If she did . . . well, she might just swoon beneath the enormity of it all!

Imagine.

She, who had never, *ever,* allowed any man near her for longer than was necessary, had actually found herself melting in Julian's arms, returning his kisses.

Veronica sharply reminded herself she'd been in shock from the dogs, her mission, and the report of Shelton's blunderbuss. Though she'd compromised herself, no one save herself and Julian knew the truth. And who would the man be telling, anyway?

No one, of course.

He clearly had something to hide, and was known as a lowly Riverkeep, to boot. If he ever *did* repeat his tale of meeting a daughter of Earl Wrothram's at Fountains, he could not possibly tell it to any one worth note.

Her secret moments of shameless indiscretion would remain just that. A secret.

As for the package she sought, Veronica believed wholeheartedly the man would search for it. For some inexplicable, stupid, foolish reason, Veronica trusted Julian would search the abbey and would keep an eye out for anyone who might place the packet there this night.

Veronica now felt a bit better, having gone over all the facts in her mind. She began to relax. She unbuttoned her short-waisted spencer, looking about her.

The bed of her rented room was ridiculously large. Obviously this inn had been constructed at a time when travelers of the road invariably shared a bed with strangers.

Veronica's face flushed at the thought.

She glanced at the curtained window, her mind skirting back to Fountains. To Julian.

What type of bed had he fashioned for himself in those ruins? Could he truly have made a home in the prisons, of all places?

Lord, but she hoped not.

She paced about the apartment, wondering when her maid would return, and what, exactly, her coachman would share with her tyrant of a father upon the earl's return from having taken the waters at Bath.

Living in a fishbowl as she did had made Veronica feel at sixes and nines. Always. If it was not her father watching her every step, it was the many servants he employed who did the deed for him. Veronica felt as though she had no peace or privacy—which she didn't.

Nettie returned a short while later, followed by buckets of steaming water carted up the inn's back stairs from the kitchen.

Once the water was delivered and poured and the door shut, Veronica set to the task of getting undressed, Nettie helping her.

"I've the antiseptic you asked fer, m'lady. A-a doctor from a place called Edinburgh was downstairs when I

asked and 'anded me this bottle, sayin' it is—is tinct're
of I-o-din. Said the bottle is yers, m'lady.''

Veronica took up the medicine, noting that the liquid was of a brownish hue. "A doctor from Edinburgh,
you say?''

Nettie nodded.

Veronica undid the bandage, revealing the nasty
scrape in her skin. She winced at the sight of it. Nettie,
however, was thankfully mum. Veronica applied the
tincture of iodine, making a mental note to later send
Nettie downstairs with payment for the good doctor.

The stinging brown liquid stained her skin. Veronica gritted her back teeth together. *"Blast,"* she muttered.

"M'lady?" her abigail asked.

"I am fine, Nettie. It merely stings, is all." Her ministrations complete, Veronica handed the medicinal
bottle back to her maid. She pinned up her own hair
while waiting for the antiseptic to have a chance at
cleansing her injury. She then sank down into the tub-
ful of steaming water, glad enough to feel the warm
water edge away all the pains and stains of her travels
to Fountains and back.

Much later, dressed in a fresh gown of spotted muslin and carrying a light shawl, with her hair repaired
and neatly pinned by Nettie, Veronica went downstairs
to the private parlour she'd requested to be reserved.
It appeared she'd been awarded the coffee room, now
cleared of customers.

Shelton was standing at the door. "I shall stand
watch while you dine, m'lady," he said, his tone indicating that not even wild horses would budge him
from the doorway.

Veronica was about to tell him that wouldn't be necessary as she was wondering if Julian might make an
appearance with word about the package. But she

knew her coachman would not be coaxed away, and in truth, the sounds coming from the occupants of the nearby taproom and from the revelers out in the street of the village made Veronica realize it was best to have Shelton nearby.

The celebration of Midsummer's Eve had taken on a decided intensity during her ablutions, no doubt with many of the partygoers nearing a tipsy mood. From the raucous noise inside the taproom, Veronica deduced she'd be getting little sleep this night—not that she would have slept anyway. If Julian did not send word about the packet, Veronica would have to devise another plan to get to Fountains.

Once inside the room, she found that the long deal table, much moisture ringed and knicked with wear, had been set for one. Veronica, too on nerves to dine alone, asked that another place be set and informed Nettie she'd be dining with her. The abigail nodded, her eyes wide as she clearly wondered what was on her lady's mind.

The answer, of course, was Julian and that dratted packet bound for Pamela's Lord Rathbone.

Veronica wondered how her rescuer fared in his quest to help locate the packet—if, indeed, he was even searching for it at all.

Six

Julian, standing atop the highest reaches of Fountains, watched until the lantern lights of Veronica and her companions receded into the distance. The mist and darkness seemed to swallow them as they headed back to the village. Clouds were skirting in, causing the moon's white glow to become fitful. Soon it and the stars would be hidden from view.

Alone at Fountains once again, Julian sat down on the ledge of stonework, stretching his long legs out in front of him.

He relished the slight noise his heels made scraping against the crumbles of small rocks . . . appreciated every whisper of the wind rustling through the grasses of the meadows below . . . and even smiled wryly at the sounds of the wild dogs, not so far off in the distance, baying mournfully. Having his hearing fully restored was a gift Julian had not been expecting, though it was one he'd fervently prayed for these past many months.

He tipped his head back against a piece of stone that had once held a heavy-leaded windowpane. Every vibration channeling through his ears to his brain was richly sweet, and Julian allowed himself a moment to simply drink it all in. The great height of where he sat did not bother him, nor did the further press of mists now creeping down in earnest from the farflung moors. This night, it seemed, nothing could unsettle him.

Except, of course, the memory of Lady Veronica. The scent and feel of her was still fresh in his mind. It would likely take a lifetime or two to erase it, Julian wagered . . . and he doubted he would *ever* forget the honeyed taste of her.

A wave of heat seized him as he recalled just how sweet kissing her had been. After they'd tumbled down the ledge and he'd cracked his skull soundly on the rocks, Julian had awakened to find his hearing restored and Veronica's lovely body atop his own. Both realizations had rocked him with such profound emotion that he'd kissed her—and hungrily, at that. He had even delved his tongue inside her mouth to taste fully of the woman and of the overwhelming moment of hearing again after ten horrible months of silence.

His behavior with the lady had been far from gentlemanly, yet she had not slapped him away as she had had every right to do, but had instead returned his kisses with innocent ardor. Her sweet abandonment in the heat of the moment had aroused Julian no small amount. If not for the second report of her man's gun, who knew where those kisses would have led them?

Julian looked up at the few remaining stars to be seen, his black gaze narrowing as he mulled over the rest of the evening's events. The beautiful gel had said she was embroiled in a mission of some sort. What had it been? Ah, yes, he thought, remembering now.

A "Venus Mission," she'd said.

Venus. What an intriguing tag for one to attach to one's duty. Venus, like the Greek Aphrodite, was, afterall, a goddess of love. Could it be that the lady's mission had something to do with matters of the heart? *Hers,* specifically?

And was this person, for whom Veronica sought the package, a man who had perhaps stolen her heart?

The very notion that Veronica might be in love with some spineless gentleman who chose to stay comfortably in Town while she sojourned to Yorkshire on his behalf disturbed Julian.

The possibility that she may have shared her ardor with this faceless beau disturbed him even more.

Agitated by the train of his thoughts, Julian turned his mind to the other startling thing she'd said to him: that she was willing to pay handsomely for his help. A position of employment, to be exact, at one of her father's many estates.

Clearly, the lady thought him to be nothing more than a luckless vagabond with no steady income, and who could fault her for that assumption? He wasn't exactly acting or looking civilized these days, and he hadn't in too long a while.

Julian's eyes hooded. He wondered what Lady Veronica's reaction would be if she ever learned that she had offered such positions as gardener, stable help, and groundskeeper to one Julian Andrew Maxmillian Masters, the seventh Earl of Eve.

The circumstances of Julian's ascension to his distinguished title were a memory right out of hell. The night the title became his was one that would be forever burned in his soul.

His mood turning black as he recalled the exact moment he became Earl of Eve, Julian got to his feet and rifled one strong hand through the shagged lengths of his dark hair. He needed a shave and a haircut, but he'd vowed not to do either until the day he uncovered the vile culprit who had torn his life asunder.

Now that his hearing was restored, he could get on with that grave matter. He'd waited ten long months for this moment and was eager to be gone from Fountains and the desolate existence he'd known here. He needed to speak in person with the two remaining people in this world whom he trusted: his solicitor in London and his manservant, Garn.

But before he vacated Fountains, Julian knew he'd be making one last round of her ruinous grounds. He would, blast it all, search for the packet the lovely Veronica was so keen on discovering. He owed her that much, at least, for his graceless ravishment of her soft mouth.

Just as he turned to head for a way down off the ledge, Julian spied some movement—a small shadowy figure—near the abbey's outer walls to the north. Julian eased back into the darkness near the window, losing himself in the blackness there.

The figure darted quickly under an archway leading inside the abbey's great hall below and then, scanning the area around and seeing no one, reached into the folds of his threadbare coat.

It was the figure of a lad, Julian noted. Probably no more than twelve years of age. And scrawny, to boot, but fleet—like the urchins inhabiting New Bond Street who were always ready to pick a deep pocket or two.

The lad withdrew a small bundle, bent down, and quickly stuffed it into the base of a pillar where the masonry had begun to crumble.

Julian stepped out of the shadows. "Ho! You, there!" he shouted.

The urchin looked up, freezing in midmotion for the fraction of a second. He seemed to be terrified by the mist threading about his legs, by the desolateness of Fountains and by the sudden appearance of a stranger when he'd thought to be alone in the great, hulking ruins. Eyes growing wide, the lad backed away from the pillar, falling to his rump as he did so, then skittering backward like a crab until, at last, he gained his footing. Once he did, he turned and ran.

Julian, long since in motion and now nearly to the ground, jumped the last few feet from the heights he'd just traversed. As soon as his feet hit the ground, he started running, hoping to head the lad off before he could escape. Julian had a few questions to ask the boy: namely, for whom the package was destined and whence it had come.

But the lad, quick and tiny, navigated the area of Fountains better than Julian ever had, and he was soon lost in the mist that had, within the last few minutes, grown knee-high to Julian's frame.

"Bloody hell," Julian said.

He knew he'd not be finding the boy now. The lad had had too much of a head start before him.

Hoping the urchin didn't come to harm—or worse, meet up with the wild dogs—Julian doubled back, heading for the pillar where the boy had tucked away the package.

Julian had it in his hands in a matter of moments. The thing was small, bound with twine and wrapped tight in sheepskin. There was nothing to note for whom the packet had been placed here or who had sent the boy to deliver it.

As Julian surveyed the package a premonition whipped up his spine, causing the hairs at the back of his neck to tingle. He knew a strong sensation that there was yet another intruder about.

Gad, who and his brother *wasn't* at Fountains this night? he wondered.

His gaze surveyed the misty area, and though he saw no one his gut instincts told him he was not alone.

Holding the bundle tight in one fist, Julian darted for the relative cover of one of the abbey's walls. Out of the corner of his right eye, he spied the shadow of a figure. The person waved one arm—quickly, as though directing the course of another—then drew back into the shadows.

Damn. There was more than just one other person about.

Reaching the wall, Julian pressed beside it, then began to inch his way to the opening of what was once a door. Just as he reached it, intending to steal through, a strong, behemoth of a man rounded it, ramming hard into Julian with his bull-like shoulder, forcing him back against the stone.

Quick as a flash, the brute slammed one meaty fist into Julian's right eye, another into his midsection, then grabbed him by the hair, yanking up his head when Julian would have doubled over from lack of air, and slammed his head back against the stone.

"Eyenin', cove," he said, a feral gleam in his mud-brown eyes, his breath reeking of rot. "It be Fate come visitin' this night." He rammed his mighty knee into Julian's groin, then grabbed Julian by the neck, hitting his head against the stone, again, again, and then a third time.

Pain exploded in Julian's brain, and the brute's ugly face swam before his eyes. To his credit, Julian didn't black out, though he feared he would if the bastard continued his murderous assault.

A second marauder stepped out of the mist.

The brute glanced back at his companion. "He's got it, Nate. Right here in his hand," he said.

The bundle—they were after the bloody bundle!

Julian briefly considered handing it over lest this brute's beating destroy his hearing—or worse. But a vision of Veronica swept through his mind, and Julian instinctively tightened his hand about the sheepskin, deciding these two miscreants could go to Jericho.

The second marauder noted Julian's reaction. "Relax, cove," he said. "It ain't the bundle we wants. We already had a look-see inside when we hauled 'at snivelin' lad off the stagecoach w' it an' tol' him he'd be hog feed if he didn't leads us t' where he was t' place it t'night. No, it was the bloke comin' to reach for 'at package what's we want'd." He smiled malevolently. "Guess, 'at would be, *you* eh, cove?"

"Who the devil are you?" Julian demanded.

"Shut yer trap and listen up," said the burly brute of the punishing fists and accurate knee.

To bring his point home, the vile being brought up one elbow and slammed it into Julian's mouth, splitting his lip open, at the same time ramming his other fist up against the underside of his chin. Julian's head snapped back, his back teeth piercing his tongue.

Julian stifled a grunt of pain. Blood immediately spilled from his split lip and trickled from the corner of his mouth while his right eye, having been bashed earlier, began to swell.

"Don't much matter who we are, cove," said the man called Nate. "Findin' somethin' what's missin' is all we're tryin' t' do. Now you just best make it easy on yerself and tell us where 'at 'spensive baubble be hidd'n. A lotta blunt be paid fer it, and our employer, 'e don't take kindly t' bein' hoax'd."

Julian, dazed now and wondering how he would extricate himself from these ruffians, stared blear eyed at the fiends. "I . . . I don't know . . . wh-what you're talking about, you swine."

"Sure'n y' do, cove. We wants 'at diamon'."

"D-diamond?" Julian felt his insides convulse at mention of a diamond.

"Aye. We wants t' bauble. And now, if y' please, 'and it ov'r or be leadin' us t' it's hidin' place. I won't be askin' so nice like ag'n."

No doubt you won't, Julian thought, inwardly cursing the scurvy lout, *because I won't give you the chance to do so.*

As they had their exchange, Julian made a pretense of coming in and out of consciousness—which wasn't, in actuality, a difficult thing to do.

He let his head loll forward, then jerked it back up. "D–don't know wh-what you're talking about," he muttered, all the while keeping a keen tally on the brute's hold of him. The oaf's grip lessened a bit as Julian pretended to lean against the stone for support.

It proved enough of a window of opportunity.

Julian took that moment to react. Suddenly coming to life, eyes blazing, he brought up his right hand— Veronica's bundle still held fast in his grip—and laid a sharp, lightning-fast blow to the man's ugly mug. He followed it with a mighty left hit to the man's temple, one meant to extinguish his lights. The great giant fell back, knocked out cold.

Julian wasted no time. He sprang forward, bending slightly, and charged toward Nate with a snarled curse. He crashed into the man's wiry body with a thundering energy, toppling him to the ground and pinning him there. Julian wanted blood.

"Tell me," he demanded, the fingers of his large left hand splayed open against the man's throat and squeezing hard, "who sent you here?"

Nate, his bravery suddenly knocked out of him as his accomplice lay still on the ground nearby, shriveled into a fearful mass of quaking limbs. "I-I know not," he gasped. "It—it be God's truth, cove, I swears! S– some lawy'r type hir'd Scruggs an' me, though we nev'r met 'im face-t'-face. We was hir'd t' come t' Yorksh'r and follow 'at snivelin' lad. We was t'ld t' beat the tar outta whoever laid claim t' 'at bundle ye ain't be lettin' go of. 'At's all I know, cove. Don't know 'at lawy'r fella, or ev'n 'is name. Scruggs an' me, we get hir'd on through sever'l messengers. We never knows the blokes what hire us, 'at be the truth, cove. I swear on me mum's grave, 'at's all I know."

Julian believed him.

Lord, into what kind of coil had Veronica enmeshed herself? He imagined the ugly scenario that would have taken place had she actually been present to discover the packet within Fountains.

On the heels of that came yet another thought . . . one that twisted Julian's gut even more.

What if a solicitor of one Lady Veronica had been the very person to orchestrate all of this, and on *her* order?

Could this be a plot to uncover him? Might the lovely Veronica actually know of what had transpired on the night he'd ascended to his title as Earl of Eve?

God, he hoped not. Prayed not.

Julian wanted to slam a fist into Nate's face, but quickly tamped down such an urge. Instead he said, each word spaced for maximum emphasis, "Know this, you swine. I've blunt enough and the sheer tenacity to dog you and your friend over there until your dying days if you ever dare come near me again. Leave this place . . . and send a message to whoever hired you that you failed miserably at your deed."

Nate swallowed thickly in the face of Julian's fury. "Aye. Right, cove. Got it, 'at I do. Ev'ry w'rd."

Julian got to his feet. "I hope you do," he muttered darkly.

Twenty minutes later, after having dropped down again into the earthen caves he'd discovered beneath Fountains, gathering up his sparse belongings from the prisons, and then retrieving his giant stallion from a private spot near the River Skell, Julian was ready to head for the Cock and Dove Inn and one Lady Veronica, who dwelled there.

But first . . .

Julian looked down at the bundle he still held tight in his right fist.

Nate had muttered something about a diamond.

God, but could he have been talking about the very same one Julian had given to his father on that fateful night long ago?

Julian untied the twine, pulled back the layer of sheepskin, and felt a thud of dread drop to the pit of his stomach.

Inside the skin lay a familiar-looking chess piece. A horseman, to be exact, fashioned of black ivory.

Julian drew in a deep breath.

Ten months ago he'd returned from the coast of Africa, bearing with him a black ivory chess set, each piece based with pure gold, for his father, the sixth Earl of Eve. Tucked inside one of those pieces had been a perfectly cut blue diamond of extraordinary size—a diamond Julian himself had carved out of the earth during his travels abroad and had used the Eve Diamond. He'd taken it back to London as a gift for his beloved father, in celebration of the man's forty-fifth natal day celebration.

But an explosion had rocked his family's house in Hanover Square that night, killing the earl, Julian's mother, and his young sister, Suzanne, and leaving Julian with his sense of hearing gone.

It had been his manservant, Garn, who had dragged Julian out of the flaming structure, saving his life. And it had been Garn who, several weeks later after Julian's bruises had healed but it seemed apparent his hearing would not be restored as easily, had reluctantly agreed to leave Julian at the ruins of Fountains, a place where

Julian and his parents had come when he was young—a place where Julian thought he might be able to heal . . . and if not that, to rot.

It all felt like a lifetime ago, yet the pain of that night had never left Julian and never would.

He turned the chess piece in his hand, noting a knick in the ivory near the gold base. Someone had pried the base off at one time. Julian did so now. Tucked inside was a piece of vellum, with a note scrawled across it.

I want the diamond and the chess set. Deliver them to me or suffer the consequences.

Julian's entire body felt suddenly as though it had been frozen on ice. Whoever had hired Nate and Scruggs through an intricate chain of lowly messengers clearly knew about Julian, the Eve Diamond, and the chess set he'd brought back to England . . . and, more importantly, doubtless had a connection to the explosion in Hanover Square that had claimed the lives of his beloved family.

B'God, but they would pay. And dearly.

Julian shoved the note back inside the horseman, reaffixed the gold base, then bundled it all with the fleecy sheepskin and twine.

Eyes filled with a burning light, he shoved the bundle into his saddle pouch, then swung his lean body astride his powerful horse. He was eager to reach the Cock and Dove Inn and one Lady Veronica. The beautiful lady had a lot of explaining to do.

And Julian would, he vowed, get the full truth from her this time.

Seven

Veronica had just pushed away a small plate of spicy Yorkshire parkin when she thought she heard some new commotion outside the coffee room door.

"M'lady," said Nettie, oblivious to the noise that had gained her lady's attention, "if you not be wantin' 'at slice of parkin, I'll gladly take it. I'm 'at hungry, I vow."

"What? Oh. Yes, of course. Help yourself, Nettie. Please, do," said a distracted Veronica, turning in her chair and straining to make out the voices beyond the door. But the din within the taproom and outside the inn had grown to such a clatter that Veronica could not separate one set of voices from another.

Perhaps what she'd heard had been nothing more than Shelton conversing with one of the revelers who'd chanced to walk by.

Blast, but she was on edge, what with wondering whether or not anyone had gone to Fountains to deliver the packet, or if Julian had begun a search for it—or if he was now finding his way to her, through the darkness the guide, Drubbs, had said he preferred over daylight.

Veronica turned back to her maid and tried to relax as she watched the girl begin a serious endeavour to devour the slice of too-spicy parkin. After the huge meal just served it was a wonder her maid had room for more. The girl had eaten not only a large serving of rabbit pie and Yorkshire pudding, but had also partaken of a healthy serving of the fried lamb's liver with golden onions—the very dish Veronica had chosen but only picked at. A tea tray had also been delivered to the table, and with it teacakes and parkin. The innkeeper had obviously ordered his cook to spare nothing for Lady Veronica.

There came a loud, angry voice from beyond the door, causing Nettie to jump in her seat and Veronica to stiffen.

That it was Shelton shouting at someone was unmistakable.

"La, m'lady," said Nettie, around the food in her mouth, "but 'e be soundin' frightful angry. Whut ev'r could be the matt'r?"

Veronica could wager a fair guess. She did not, however, have a chance to go and see for herself.

Within seconds, the coffee room door was thrust open and the cause of Shelton's ill-tempered shouts made his presence known.

"Julian," breathed Veronica.

"Lawks!" shrieked Nettie, nearly choking on her food at sight of the bloodied but still handsome intruder. The maid jumped to her feet, upending her chair, then plastered her body back against the far wall, where she stayed, shivering in complete and utter terror at the man's ungentlemanly entrance . . . and then, by degrees, she relaxed her stance as she got a good view of his rugged, handsome face and his deep darkling eyes.

Veronica, too, would have liked to jump back and away from the man, but instinctively knew he would not allow any such thing. By the savage look in his black gaze, Julian had come to see her head on a platter.

And by the looks of his battered face, he'd met with trouble after she'd left him at Fountains.

"Dearest God," Veronica whispered at the sight of him. A thousand questions tumbled through her brain.

Shelton came charging in after Julian. "I tell you again, man, *get out!* Lest you want the innkeep and constable alerted and ordered to drag you gone by your ears you will leave *now!* Do you hear?"

"Aye. I hear you," muttered Julian, who had eyes only for Veronica.

She paled. His right eye was swollen and grotesque, his lip split and bleeding into the hairs of his beard. Good heavens, what had transpired at the abbey after she'd gone?

"Tell your man and your maid to leave us," Julian said, so softly that Veronica had to strain to hear him. "You and I have much to discuss, my lady." He made a slight movement with his right hand.

Veronica dropped her gaze, her eyes widening at sight of a small bundle of sheepskin bound with twine that he held in his fist. She gave him an almost imperceptible nod of her head, then looked first at Nettie and then to Shelton. "I would have a word with this man. Alone. Please leave us."

Nettie's eyes nearly popped out of her head. "Awks! You *know* him, m'lady?"

"Nettie," Veronica said, a warning tone in her voice.

"Wh-what I meant to say, m'lady, is . . . well . . . are you certain sure you want to be *alone* with him?"

"Very certain, Nettie. Now go."

The maid, clearly at an inner crossroads, decided finally she'd best bite her tongue and leave her lady to her business. "Well, if 'n yer certain," she muttered.

She left her place at the wall, grabbed up one of the remaining Yorkshire teacakes from a plate near the parkin on the deal table, then scurried out of the room—but not before casting one last lingering glance at the tall, bearded fellow who'd invaded the chamber and who seemed mighty interested in having a private audience with her lady.

Shelton proved not so easy to dismiss.

" 'Tis out of the question," he proclaimed loudly. He cast Julian a withering glance. "I'll not be leaving you to such a vagabond as this, my lady," he declared. "The earl would not be pleased. He would—"

"Leave us, Shelton," Veronica cut in, her tone brooking no argument. It took every ounce of her daring to stand up to her father's most trusted servant, but she did so unwaveringly. The bundle in Julian's hands, and the bruises to his face, were enough of an incentive. And, too, a small voice in her soul whispered, this is what she'd wanted, after all, when he'd left her, slipping into the dark mouth of that earthen cave. She'd known then, as she knew now, that she very much wanted to be alone with this man again.

Shelton muttered something unintelligible, and then, with a baleful glare at Julian, finally relented. "Aye, my lady. As you deem," he muttered, scowling. "But do know I shall plant myself on the other side of this door. And do know I'll not be allowing this private audience to go on too long."

With that, Shelton let himself out, reluctantly shutting the portal behind him.

Veronica let out a breath. *"Gad,"* she whispered, her gaze once again sweeping over Julian's bruised and battered face.

"Moody, ugly brute of a fellow, isn't he?" Julian commented.

Veronica clicked her tongue, getting to her feet. "And what did you expect? You look like the wrath of

God. Indeed, it appears as though someone made a boxing bag of your face."

"How perceptive of you. Someone, in fact, did just that, my lady. And the rest of my body, to boot."

Veronica winced, both at his intended sarcasm and at the thought of the pain he must have been in, at the very thought of him being beaten.

"Please, have a seat," she insisted.

"Afraid I might swoon at your feet?"

"What I am afraid of is that you might bleed a river if you don't soon sit down and let your heart still to a normal beat," Veronica said pragmatically. "Good Lord, what happened? Your lip looks as though it was split open by a hammer—and your *eye* . . . it is swelling and turning purple even as we speak."

Julian, not a little incensed, forcefully placed the bundle he held down atop the deal table. "What happened," he said darkly, "is *this.*"

Veronica swallowed past the sudden lump of dread in her throat as she looked down at the sheepskin-wrapped bundled. *"My package?"*

"Aye."

Veronica returned her gaze to his. "Julian, you—you were beaten because of this? But why . . . why would anyone do such a thing?"

"You tell *me,"* he said. "I was nearly beaten to a pulp because I held that thing in my hand."

Veronica felt pure fear flutter in her breast. For the first time since beginning her Venus Mission she was truly frightened at what she might have gotten herself into—and Julian, as well—by intercepting Lord Rathbone's delivery.

She stared at Julian, at his cut and bruised face. "Are—are you saying that whoever left this at Fountains did this to you?"

He shook his head, and a small wave of relief washed

through Veronica. It was quickly swept away, however, when he said, "It was but a lad who left the package, my lady. He tucked it into a crevice of the stones and then ran. It was the two hulking brutes who'd followed him that did the deed."

"Good heavens," Veronica breathed.

There had been someone following the messenger? Good Lord and good Lord, but she and Pamela had never considered such a possibility when they'd hatched their wild scheme. Come to think of it, they had not considered much of anything other than getting Veronica to Fountains to look for a package to be placed there at the height of Midsummer's Eve. All in all, their Venus Mission lacked a great deal of forethought, Veronica decided miserably.

And now this.

Veronica looked again at Julian, feeling a miserable sick feeling in the pit of her stomach at the sight of his battered features. As she did so, he swayed once—a clue that he was not bearing up as well to his punishing beating as he'd like to think he was.

Veronica instantly moved into action. "I must insist that you sit down, sir. In another moment, I fear you're going to topple like a fallen tree," she said, turning her chair about and indicating for him to sit.

"The deuce I will," he muttered, glowering at her. "I want some answers, Lady Veronica. I want them now."

"Yes, yes, of course you do. As do I," she said, trying her best to soothe his ire. "And we shall muddle through all the facts that we have, sir, in just a moment. But first you must sit down and tend to your cuts."

"The devil I must! What I *will* do is—"

He stopped his spate of words as Veronica, both hands against his shoulders, bodily forced him down atop the chair. *"Sit down, Julian."*

He went down with a solid thud, the wood of the hard chair creaking beneath his weight.

"I am not one of your hired hands to be ordered about," he muttered, glaring at her with his uninjured eye.

"Of course you are not, sir," Veronica said. "And by the bye, I do not order my servants about." *If anything,* she thought to herself, *it is surely the other way around.*

She'd already turned to the deal table. She picked up a napkin, then opened the pot of hot water that the waiter had brought earlier with the tea tray. The steam had long since gone, but the water had been boiled and so would be suitable to clean Julian's cuts. Having dipped the linen napkin into the pot, she turned back toward him.

"May I?" she asked.

He was still glaring at her with his uninjured eye, but some of the fight, it seemed, had drained out of him now that he'd sat down.

"I've come to the conclusion, my lady, that you do as you please. Always."

Veronica ignored the rub. She dabbed gingerly at his cut lip. He jerked a bit, no doubt from the sting. "I hear there is a doctor from Edinburgh on the premises," she said quietly.

"Not interested," he muttered around the square of moistened linen.

Veronica went on doggedly. "I received a bottle of antiseptic from him for my injury. Tincture of iodine, it is called."

He lifted one brow, the light in his good eye softening. "How *is* your wound?"

"Not nearly as bad as yours and pray, sir, do not try and change the subject."

"I'm not."

"I can send someone to find this doctor, Julian," Veronica went on. "He could tend to you, could have a look at these cuts and—"

"No."

She could tell by the tone of his voice there was little sense in arguing the point. Still, however, Veronica decided she'd try one last tactic.

"And what about your hearing?" she demanded, not pausing in her ministrations, not even when she felt his lean, whipcord body stiffen. " 'Tis obvious you've suffered several blows to your head, Julian. Are you so foolish as to believe they might not have affected your sense of hearing?"

He reached up with his right arm, capturing her finely-shaped hand in his large, roughened one. "What *about* my hearing?" he demanded. "Just exactly what do you know, my lady?"

Veronica tamped down a gasp at his manhandling of her. She *would not* react to him with fear, she told herself sternly, for clearly that was his ploy: to startle and subdue her by his sheer strength.

"Relax, sir. The truth of the matter is, I know very little." Letting out a breath, Veronica jerked her hand from his, turned the napkin about. Then she placed a clean edge of it into the teakettle and began again to clear the blood from his lip. "The man who led my coachman to the abbey told me a bit about you—or rather, the legend of you."

"Legend? What the deuce does that mean?"

"You've become known as 'The Riverkeep,' sir. It . . . it appears you have frightened all of the locals in this shire, and they've decided you are something betwixt a demon and a specter, what with your lurking about that ruinous abbey and coming out only in the depths of night. It is also claimed you are deaf—if indeed a demon or a specter can be such a thing." She dabbed at the last of the blood on his mouth, then straightened. "I believe only in the part about your deafness, if you must know."

He was silent as he gazed up at her.

Veronica forced herself to continue, to say what was on her mind. "You couldn't hear a thing when you first met me at Fountains, could you, Julian? It was only when you thrust us over that ledge, and hit your head during our fall, that your hearing was restored. That's why, when you first opened your eyes, there were tears in them—and that is why you whispered to me that I was your 'hope and need answered,' isn't it?"

He obviously did not like the train of her words, but Veronica refused to stop.

"Tell me, Julian," she said, "have you lived at Fountains for these past many months because you felt as ruined as her walls, as empty and as void as her once-rich lands?"

"God," he breathed. He sucked in a harsh breath, frowning. "Don't ask me these things."

"Why not? What are you hiding, Julian? Or should I ask from *whom* are you hiding?"

It was the wrong question. Like a bolt of lightning, Julian shot up from the chair, seized her by her upper arms, and held her fast, his battered face just inches from her own.

"You ask a lot of questions for someone who seems to have her own secrets to keep hidden, my lady." His face twisting with anger, he nodded to the package still on the table—one Veronica hadn't even bothered to open. "Care to explain to me why you haven't unwrapped that bundle, the one you were so bloody intent on finding?"

Veronica, tears of fear smarting behind her eyes, reacted to his brutality in the only way she knew how:

with anger. In fact, a lifetime of being verbally and sometimes physically abused by her father came rushing to the forefront, overwhelming her with such a heated frenzy that she pushed the man away. "No, I'll *not* be telling you," she spat, "because it is not your affair, and I'll not be bullied by the likes of you, sir!"

To Veronica's amazement, he did not reach for her again. Instead, he stared at her hard, his good eye full of dark portent and his ravaged eye looking twice as menacing.

"By the likes of me?" he repeated. "Does that mean you find me beneath you, *my lady*—beneath even the coachman and maid you order about with such little feeling?"

"Blast you," Veronica replied. She was surprised at the rancor of her voice, at the pure fury now beating in her breast. "You know nothing about me. Nothing about my life, sir!"

"No, I don't, but I can guess. For the most part, you're a pampered belle, living a queen's existence, and you obviously think the world and its brother should bow at your feet, allowing you your every wish and whim."

How very wrong he was! Veronica would have liked to give him a scathing set down—indeed, she'd have reveled in slapping him soundly for such crude words.

But Veronica had had enough of physical violence to last a lifetime, thanks to her father. And in truth, she could never, ever raise her hand to another human being—and certainly not to this man.

Taking a deep breath, and praying for some composure, Veronica took the bundle off the deal table, and then looked the man straight in the face.

"Regardless of what you think of me, sir, do know I am sorry for whatever happened at Fountains this night. I-I had asked you to help locate this package for me, promising employment in return. You have done just that. I appreciate your help and I wish you Godspeed. I don't care what you're running from and I don't care to find out. Trust me when I say I shall not utter a word about any of this to anyone. And now if you'll excuse me, I think it is time I take my leave."

He remained silent, simply watching her.

Veronica felt ill at ease beneath his scrutiny. In her mind, a tumble of scenarios played themselves out. She'd promised him payment in the form of employment. Dared she do just that? Her father would question her mercilessly—and no doubt just as mercilessly reject her request of hiring on some man she'd met in Yorkshire. Gad, how would she even broach the subject to the earl?

In the next instant, Veronica knew she would never dare do such a thing. If she could, she would simply arrange the man's employment on her own, at one of her father's most far-flung estates, at that. And then she would pray mightily that the earl would not be visiting that estate any time soon.

Gad, what had she gotten herself into? She'd never really meant to betray this stranger with an empty promise—she'd simply been desperate to have Rathbone's package. And since Julian had appeared so down and out of luck and in need of employment, like a ninny had dangled the carrot of a job and a roof over his head to lure him into helping her.

And now, unfortunately, it was time to pay. . . .

Veronica inwardly winced. She felt as though she was stuck fast betwixt a rock and a hard place. To actually find employment for him would lead, eventually, to Earl Wrothram learning the full of her sojourn to Yorkshire and her meeting with Julian.

In a rash, reckless moment, Veronica made her decision. "If you give me an address, I'll post word to you of where and what your employment will be in payment of your services this night," she announced.

The truth of it was, Veronica had no intention of doing any such thing. She would, however, she decided, sell some of her jewels and perhaps even try to get at some of the inheritance her maternal grandmother had left her. She would ensure that a tidy sum of money was given to Julian for his deeds this night, no matter the cost to her own future security.

It would have to serve as balm enough.

Julian, though, seemed to have a sixth sense where her thoughts were concerned.

With alarming speed and strength, he reached out, grabbed her by her upper arms, and then carefully but with purpose plopped her down atop the chair he'd just vacated. That done, he fastened his fists about the tall back of the chair, leaned down, and met her startled gaze with his own fierce one.

His face nearly touching hers, he said, lowly, darkly, "The position I desire is not at some far-flung estate of your father's, Veronica, but at the very one where *you* reside. And the job I will be employed to do will not be in any Town garden or some crowded mews, but acting as your personal guard, whether you like it or not."

Veronica blinked in dismay.

Julian was not about to be hampered in his speech. Ignoring her reaction, he said, "That package you left me to find is something akin to a bloody Pandora's box. Because of it . . . and because of your plea for me to find it, I was nearly beaten to death. And I've no doubt, my lady, but the two river rats who accosted me this night might soon be in pursuit of you . . . unless, of course," he added, his voice going low, accusatory in tone, "*you* are the one who employed them."

Veronica sucked in a gasp. "Do not be absurd!"

"I am not. If anything, I am being careful."

"But I know nothing of the men who accosted you! Indeed, if you must know the truth, I-I know very little about the package you found, other than the fact it is destined for a well-heeled lord in Town," Veronica said, her words tumbling out.

The look in his ravaged face told her he believed that much. "And is this lord in Town a friend of yours?" he demanded.

No, Veronica thought, thinking of the blond-haired Rathbone with his silky smile and empty phrases.

But in the next instant, she thought of Pamela, and of how much the pretty and true Pam had helped her during that first year in London when Veronica had been at sixes and nines in worrying over the too-lovely Lily and her sister's penchant to fall in love and give her all to every rake who came her way.

For Pamela, Veronica would do anything. Even lie to this dangerous stranger who had been a help.

"Yes," she heard herself whisper, "this person is a dear, dear friend of mine."

Her words seemed to seal Julian's resolve. "The matter is settled then," he said.

"What?" Veronica cried. "Nothing is settled, sir, other than that I will indeed pay you for your trouble and—"

"You heard me," he cut in, then motioned with a slight nod of his head toward the door. "Tell your man you'll be leaving this inn at dawn. Explain to him I will be accompanying you, will now be your personal guard. Do not allow him to overstay your rule. Is that clear, my lady?"

Veronica was aghast. "No! None of this is clear," she gasped. "It's absurd and preposterous and—"

"Do it," Julian cut in. "No matter what it takes, no matter how firm you need to be, you tell your man that I am joining you on your trip back to London and that I will be your shadow even beyond the moment you are tucked securely back in your bed there."

Veronica gaped at him, fighting hard to keep her composure. She was more than just a little affected by his mention of her bed . . . and that he'd be lingering near her at all times. "He—he will never allow it," she whispered.

"For whom does the man work?" Julian demanded. "Himself or your family?"

He works for my father only, Veronica thought, but did not say the words. "Wh-what you are proposing is outrageous. I'll be perfectly safe in my family's home in London. I—"

Roughly, he cut in, "Devil take it, my lady. You seem not to understand. Your choice in this matter is none. I *will* go with you to London, I *will* shadow your every step . . . and as God as my witness, lady, *I will put you abed myself every night if I deem it necessary.*"

Veronica gaped at him, shocked. Good Lord, but she believed him. "You are mad," she whispered.

"Aye. A specter risen from Fountains, brought out of her depths by your own hand, my lady. I'm involved now, up to my eyeteeth in this Venus Mission of yours, and not you or your coachman or the hounds of hell will stop me from doing what I vow. Now go. Tell your coachman."

Veronica knew a terror beating in her breast. What had she unleashed this night. Drat that package, and blast this—this riverkeep!

"I'll inform him," she ground out, "but once we are in London, sir, you can rest assured I'll not be heeling to *your* word."

"We'll see about that," he replied. "Now go upstairs and see that your things are packed. I'll be back within the hour."

"Wh-what do you mean, you'll be 'back?' " she asked warily.

"Just what I said. My duties as your personal guard begin this night. Do leave a light lit for me in your room."

"The devil I will!" she blasted.

But he wasn't listening. Before she could stop him he swiped the bundle from her hands and headed for the door.

"Wait!" she cried. "Where are you going with that?"

He glanced at her over one shoulder, his battered eye looking frightful. "I'm taking it with me."

"But I *need* that!"

"Aye," he muttered. "So I've noted."

"Stop. You cannot just take it with you!"

"I can and will, my lady. Call it insurance."

"Insurance for what, blast it all," Veronica demanded.

"Insurance that you won't be leaving this inn without me." He reached for the handle of the coffee room door. "I'll see you within the hour. Go straight to your room. Talk to no one other than your own servants."

With that, he thrust open the portal, ignored Shelton's huge bulk of a frame turning on him, and then was gone.

Veronica let out a furious breath. What an insufferable, arrogant, rude beast of a man! *Blast him!* she thought.

Shelton glowered at her from the doorway.

Veronica glowered right back. Gad, but she'd had enough of men this night! "We leave for London in the morning," she snapped. "At dawn. Have everything ready. I'm going to my room."

"My lady," he began in a dark tone.

"Not a word, Shelton," she said, cutting him off.

And before the man could question or gainsay her, Veronica swept past him, her mind in turmoil.

Julian intended to be her bodyguard. Gad, what a notion!

If he hadn't taken the packet with him, she'd have sighed in relief and then hurried away from Yorkshire with no qualms.

But he *had* taken the package, and now Veronica had no choice but to do as he ordained.

Her personal guard indeed. What an ogre he was. What a perfect lout! What *was* the man thinking?

But as Veronica headed deeper into the hall, away from the coffee room and her coachman, she began to grow truly edgy. It seemed that all of Yorkshire was awake and partying in earnest. Some vagabonds had obviously beaten Julian soundly. Could those miscreants have followed him to the Cock and Dove? Could they be watching now as Veronica headed upstairs to her rented chambers?

She had no idea.

Deciding not to make a target of herself, Veronica hurried up the staircase, then quickly let herself into her apartments.

Nettie was waiting for her with wide eyes.

"Lawks, m'lady," said Nettie, "I was a-feared I'd left you to the devil himself down there! Are you all right? You're not abused in any way, are you?"

Yes! she wanted to shout. *I've been abused and sorely treated and—and, blast it all, kissed until my toes curled and my heart leaped.* And that, alas, above all the others, was the sole reason why Veronica had allowed Julian his way. Not because of the danger she might be in, or even so much because of the package . . . but because he'd kissed to life something inside her that had lain dormant too long.

Somehow, someway, Julian had wormed his way into

the small space of her soul she'd kept so deeply buried all these years. It had happened the moment he'd kissed her at Fountains and when he'd claimed she was his hope and need answered.

And now . . . now he was going home with her to London, to be her personal guard.

But who would guard her from Julian?

More importantly, who would guard her heart?

Eight

Julian rode out of the village, setting his horse to a fast lope, his mind a-tumble with thoughts.

His brutish behavior with Veronica had been inexcusable, he knew, but he'd had to push her, to glean for himself whether or not she'd hired those miscreants to attack him. A part of him believed that she hadn't. He had known it the second he'd looked into her eyes, he could read the truth of her innocence in those violet depths.

But that did not mean her 'friend' in London was not without guilt, and so Julian had quickly seized upon the idea of playing her guard and following her to London.

Zounds! What a notion. Even now, he could not believe he'd actually taken such a course—but he had, and now he would see it through.

Julian did not fear being recognized by anyone of the *ton*, given that he'd fobbed off Society the year he'd graduated University and then had left England altogether, satiating his yen for travel in lieu of boring Seasons in Town.

His father had allowed him his head, given that the sixth Earl of Eve had been but ten-and-seven when Julian was born, and hale and healthy and expecting to live a long life, he'd seen no need for his only son to bother with the Marriage Mart if he had a yearning to go abroad instead. Seeing that Julian settled down and set to the task of overseeing the many holdings of the Eve fortune could come later, the earl had often told his son. And so it had been thus, and Julian had traveled, visiting his family over the years, usually at one of their country estates and only rarely in London, for his parents did not like Town life much either.

No, Julian had little fear that he'd be noticed by any peers, disguised as he was with bruises, a beard, and ten months' growth of his black hair. He would play Veronica's personal guard . . . and ferret out information about the murder of his family while doing so.

Julian had to admit it felt good to be doing something, to at last have a plan of sorts after so many months of nothing and nothingness. He'd been waiting for this very opportunity for a long, long while.

Back in the village, the many bonfires lit in celebration of Midsummer's Eve had seemed to light the night, pushing back the press of darkness and even the mist that had come threading into the village. Before he'd left Ripon, Julian had passed by a sea of faces, all of them smiling and happy—and long before he'd put his mount to a canter he'd had to pause along the lane for some revelers crossing in his path, and a young girl had reached up, handing him a small almond cake and with it the magic of summer that lit her eyes.

She'd not drawn back in fear at the sight of Julian's bearded, beaten face and shagged hair, but had merely wished to share some of her youthful joy at staying up so late and being part of such revelry, and it had occurred to him at that moment—and as it had at Fountains when he'd first heard Veronica's voice and then kissed her—that life could perhaps hold some sweetness once again, that there might, somehow, be something good to be wrought of it all. But then the girl was gone . . . the moment lost—as though it had never been.

Julian had continued along the lane, and in the next instant was wondering if Nate and Scruggs were somewhere behind him, gathered round one of the fires, if they had seen him enter or exit the inn, or if they themselves had gone into the inn, in search of Veronica.

It was that last unanswered detail that bothered him most of all. However much or how little Veronica might know about the packet, about the explosion that had taken his family from him, Julian still found himself worrying over her welfare. She had bewitched him with her violet eyes, soft curves, and even softer mouth . . . *and gad,* but her sweetly eager response to his hungry kisses had near torn his soul asunder.

Earlier, when he'd first touched her, he'd had to fight for control. He'd wanted nothing more than to take her then and there. Her lips had tasted like nectar and her body, so lithe, had felt just right in his arms. Julian could well imagine what a night with Veronica would be like: 'Twould be heaven, he wagered, and would make him want another and another. . . .

Julian rode on into the darkness, forcing away such lusty thoughts. He focused instead on the wind he could hear in his ears, on the steady, powerful beat of his horse's hooves atop the ground, and even the hoot of a far-off owl now and then.

He had a twenty-minute ride ahead of him, and twenty minutes back. It did not leave much time for all he had to say to the man he now sought . . . and no time, *absolutely none,* he told himself, for allowing his mind to drift back to those moments at the abbey when a too-beautiful, daring and determined female had come careening into his bleak existence.

The small, weather-beaten cottage with but a few

outerbuildings stood huddled in the folds of a great
sweep of sheep-cropped sod that flowed upward and
beyond, stretching out far into the darkness. Candle-
light glowed from the two small windows that faced in
the direction of Ripon.

Julian was glad to see the light. The hour was growing late and he'd wondered if he would have to rouse
the inhabitants from their beds.

He dismounted, but not before smoothing one
opened palm along the neck of his trusty bay. The
horse blew out a breath, seemingly as glad as Julian
to finally be moving and going farther than just the
lands of Fountains. During their ride here the horse
had seemed to sense his master's mission and renewed
strength, and as if he'd been storing up energy for the
past many months the animal had flown over the earth
as though he had wings.

In another moment, Julian stood before the door
of the cottage. He rapped twice with his knuckles on
its weathered wood. A shadow moved by one of the
windows, peered out around a slight lift of a curtain,
and then opened the portal.

"Hello, Garn," Julian said, seeing a brief flicker of
surprise in those familiar blue eyes. He tipped a slow
smile at the man, then said, "The owls are hooting
tonight."

"Sweet mother of—you can *hear*, m'lord!"

"Aye. I can hear, Garn. And damn glorious it is to
hear *your* voice, my friend."

"Ah, and yours, m'lord, and to see that grin on your
face—which, by the way, looks like hell, m'lord, but a
far sight better than when I first left you at Fountains."

Julian reached up and gingerly touched the skin
near his battered eye. "That bad, eh?"

"Aye, m'lord. A shiner to beat all." Garn reached
for his lordship's hand and drew him inside, quickly

shutting the door and calling out as he did so. "Meg, girl, 'tis the Earl of Eve come t' pay a visit. Step lively, sis, and maybe warm some of that stew you fussed over all the day long."

Julian held up one hand. "No, no food, Garn. I'm heading to London. That's why I'm here. We've a lot to discuss."

"London, huh? That can mean only one thing."

"Aye." Julian nodded. "I might have the barest lead to ferreting out the blackheart who murdered my family, Garn. But I'm going to need your help."

"And you'll have it, m'lord."

Just then, the door to one of the other two rooms of the cottage was whisked open, and Garn's sister, Meg, stepped out.

Julian smiled at the woman, who dropped a somewhat clumsy curtsy, given her big bones and sturdy weight, then smiled back at him. Meg was fifty if she was a day. Widowed and childless, she'd lived in this cottage all of her days and appeared content to do so until her very last minute on this earth. She raised sheep and liked to knit—though how she ever managed a pair of needles with those big, manlike hands of hers, Julian would never know. She was a good woman, and she'd welcomed her brother, Garn, back home with wide arms and no questions asked.

And she asked no questions now, not even when she saw the marks of the beating on Julian's face. She merely moved to a side cupboard in the corner of the room, fished out a small jar of some kind of salve, pulled a threadbare but clean cloth from the cubbyhole as well, then set both on the small, scarred table around which four serviceable wooden chairs were pushed in.

"For your eye, m'lord," she said simply, then

added, "And I hope whoever did this to you has two to match it."

Meg didn't linger to share idle talk.

"If you be changin' your mind about wantin' some food, m'lord, just give a holler."

With that, she headed back to her room, closing the door behind her. She'd never interfered in her brother's business with his lordship, and clearly never would. Julian had come to the conclusion that Meg probably didn't give a fig about titles or travels or anything that didn't have to do with her precious sheep and the land around her cottage, which she loved so much.

Garn pulled out a chair for Julian, waiting for him to be seated; then he hauled out a chair for himself and sat down. A short wax stub of a candle burned bright at the middle of the table, its flame dancing in the draft of air that whispered aloft with Meg's closing door.

Garn sat back and, like his sister, asked no questions. They were a family of few words but huge hearts, and Garn clearly knew that, when his lordship was ready to talk, he would talk and tell Garn what he needed to know.

Garn was fifteen years younger than his sister, of medium height, and well built, with muscles made strong by manual work. He was not at all the average sort of manservant known to tend to the gentlemen of the *ton*—which was exactly what Julian had wanted those many years ago when he'd gone searching for a servant.

Rawboned and tough as an ox, Garn had a sheaf of wheat-colored hair that continually flopped over his brow in a devil-may-care kind of way. His eyes were a bright, vivid blue, with creases at their sides, which were deepened by his time out of doors and his penchant to smile often.

Julian had met Garn ten years ago in the northernmost reaches of Yorkshire at some lowly tavern that stank of rot but held a lively, likable atmosphere. Julian was just about to be launched on his Grand Tour, but had decided to kick about the countryside for a week or two beforehand. He'd graduated University, and never much caring for the bother of London he had instead headed to his favorite area—the shires of Yorkshire.

Elbow to elbow, the heir to the Eve title had matched the brawny Garn drink for drink of the gut-burning grog the tavern was proud to serve. Within the hour, he and Garn had found a fast kinship, but hadn't yet bothered to share their names with each other. Within the second hour, they'd found themselves boxing partners when a pair of drunken locals had come in, treated the serving maid wretchedly, and seemed spoiling for a fight. Garn and Julian, thinking to help the maid out, had quickly obliged.

When it was all over, their opponents had sported a broken nose each, and Julian and Garn, with their knuckles raw from punches, had finally shook hands and introduced themselves.

If Garn had been surprised to find he'd been fighting side by side with the son of a blueblood, he made no sign of it. He merely smiled that easy smile of his, which spread all the way into his clear blue eyes, and said, matter-of-factly, "You fight fair, sir. An honest man. I like that."

Julian knew then he'd made himself a true friend. The two went back inside the tavern, and over a shared platter of bacon rolls, which the maid heaped full with extra mustard and great hunks of bacon for their chivalry on her behalf, Julian learned about Garn's life.

The man hailed from a family of meager means, his parents had long since gone to their graves. He'd fallen in love—once and only once—had married the girl, who'd been three months pregnant when he'd met her, and then had buried her on the day he turned twenty. She'd died in childbirth, leaving him a babe that wasn't his own . . . and a heart, Julian suspected, that would never let another woman into its center.

His sister, Meg, a widow, took charge of rearing the boy he'd named Wil while Garn roved about the shire, finding odd jobs where he could. He had no particular skills to speak of, he was just a roaming kind of fellow with a soul made restless perhaps by the loss of his young wife. He put in a good day's work, he'd said, and Julian had known instantly that here was a man who would never complain about his lot in life, no matter how cruel it proved to be.

Julian's father, the sixth Earl of Eve, had been muttering that, while his son need not settle down just yet and get on with the business of preparing for the title he would one day ascend, he did, however, want Julian to find himself a proper valet or manservant to tend to him during his travels. Julian decided to offer the husky and amiable Garn the position. Julian had no need for a haughty valet, but instead wanted a man in his employ whom he could trust implicitly—not only with his business, but with his life.

He'd half expected Garn to laugh and decline the offer. After all, the two of them knew Garn was in no way a 'proper' anything, and besides, this brawny fellow seemed to like his gypsy life, never rooted in one place. Maybe it was the loss of his young wife that caused him to roam. Or maybe it was just in his blood.

To Julian's amazement, Garn had looked at him, thought a moment, then nodded. "It'd be my honor, sir," he'd said. "You just show me how, and I'll be the best manservant a gentleman could ever have."

Julian had never regretted the decision made in that ill-kempt tavern. Though the earl had questioned Julian's decision at first, he'd soon come to see for himself the good qualities in Garn that his son had recognized that first moment in meeting him.

Garn had gone with Julian on his tour—and for the ten years following had stayed with him through thick and thin as Julian, ever the explorer, travelled the world and sought to see every inch of it he possibly could.

And when, on that fateful night August last, Julian's world had been blown apart, it had been the brave, brawny Garn who'd faced the flames engulfing the house in Hanover Square, hefted Julian's weight onto his own broad shoulders, and borne him to safety.

And it had been Garn who'd left his battered and deaf master at the ruins of Fountains, seeing in his lordship's eyes a bottomless grief he himself knew all too well. Garn clearly hadn't wanted to leave him there, but Julian had been adamant. And always true, Garn had obliged, knowing that a man had to deal with his demons in his own way, and his grief in the same fashion.

Garn had gone to Meg's cottage, where Wil still lived. Though Julian had told Garn many times to send for the boy and have him with them on their trips abroad, Garn had refused. Julian, respecting Garn's privacy, hadn't pushed the matter, though he did insist that Garn allow him to see that the boy was taught to read and write. Hell, Julian would have sent the lad to the finest school possible if Garn would have agreed.

But the subject of Wil was one that he could not plank with Garn, and Julian often wondered if it was because the lad reminded Garn of the young wife he'd lost too soon—or if it was because the lad was a constant reminder that he had not been his wife's first lover.

Julian knew for a fact that over the years Garn had sent a good portion of his wages back home to Meg. By the looks of the cottage, though clean and well kept, she'd done no more with the funds than clothe and feed the boy, using none of it for herself or her buildings. The bulk of that money was no doubt collecting interest in some bank Meg never bothered to contact.

Julian now dipped an end of the rag into the jar of salve Meg had left on the table. "How have you been, Garn?"

"Well, m'lord, and bidin' my time till you were the same. Though I'll be honest and say there was many a day I feared you'd just dig a grave for yourself at Fountains and lie down in it."

Julian nodded. "I won't say I didn't consider doing just that a few times, my friend." A moment of silence followed; then Julian asked, "And Wil? How does the boy fare?"

Garn gave a small grunt of a laugh, though this one didn't quite reach his eyes. "No longer a boy, he's tall as a tree and just as hard to sway."

"Oh?"

"Aye, m'lord." Garn shrugged. "At ten and five, he's worse than I ever was at that age, all full of vinegar one minute and black mood the next."

Julian nodded, remembering his own self at that age, not quite a man but wanting desperately to be treated as such. "And Meg?" he asked.

"Just as hard to sway." His voice dropped to a conspiratorial whisper. "I think she's knittin' you a scarf m'lord—one to reach to your toes and back, no doubt."

Julian laughed. "God, not *another* one," he joked good-naturedly.

"Aye. Another. And proud of it. Red, this time, as bright a red as any bleedin' sunset over those oceans you so like to travel."

Julian just shook his head, knowing full well he'd wear the damned thing, no matter how long or how ugly. "I meant to tell her that the pastries she made and you delivered to Fountains were as tasty as any I've ever had," he said.

"I'll share the message," Garn replied. He watched as Julian rubbed some of the salve to his battered eye. "How many of 'em?" he asked, his tone turning serious.

"Two," said Julian.

"They came in search of you?"

"I don't think so, though I can't prove that. Gad, Garn, but the night was hectic. Fountains, believe it or not, was as busy as any turnpike this night."

"Go on," said Garn. "I'm listenin'."

Julian winced at the sting of the salve, then, cussing beneath his breath, slopped another healthy dose of it to his swelling and tender eye. "It all began with a woman. She came looking for a package—one that was to be placed somewhere in the abbey at the height of Midsummer's Eve. Those damnable dogs reached her before I did, but I managed to get her hand in mine and pull her up from their jaws. Then the two of us went tumbling over a ledge. I struck my head during the fall, Garn. Saw stars and the whole lot, then opened my eyes and found I could hear again."

Garn nodded at that part of the story. "Thank God for women, eh?" he said—and grinned, a sad sort of grin.

Julian thought of Garn's young bride then. An image of her, of what he supposed she must have looked like, must have *been* to Garn, flitted through his brain.

"Aye, my friend," he agreed softly.

But the image of the bride long dead was soon swallowed by the memory of Veronica thundering into his brain. God, just the thought of her, of holding her, kissing her, half aroused Julian. "At least, I think so," he added in a mutter.

Julian didn't need to have his loins grow tight at mere thoughts of the reckless, headstrong Veronica, he decided violently. So thinking, he delved deeper into the jar of salve and plastered another dollop to his bruised face. The stuff smarted like hell and he told himself he was glad for the burning pain of it.

Garn raised one blond brow, clearly sensing some inner turmoil within his master—one caused by the lady, no doubt—but of course, the brawny man said nothing.

Julian scowled, suddenly not liking that he was such an open book for his friend. He endeavored to continue his story.

"Her coachman and some guide came following after her. Had a devil of a time skirting around them, but we managed it, long enough for her to tell me about the package she was after. Then a short time later what should I see but a lad—an urchin, actually, by the looks of him—coming into the abbey and placing a package in the crumbled stones of a pillar. I intended to question him, but he ran off. Two thugs showed themselves the minute I got the bundle in my hands. They thought to make mincemeat of me, but I rallied back and learned they'd been hired not to get the package, but to mangle the person who reached for it. It seems that whoever hired them did so through a tangled network of lowly miscreants."

Garn digested this information, acting no more alarmed than if he'd just been informed of the price of chickens on the day's market.

After a moment of contemplation, he asked, "And the package?"

Julian settled back in the chair, done with the salve. "It wasn't really a package, but rather a bit of sheepskin with the fleece on it—of the variety your Meg raises—and tied tight with twine."

Garn's brows lifted at that news, but he said nothing.

"And here," Julian continued, "is where the tale turns truly ugly, Garn. I pulled back the sheepskin to find a familiar chess piece—from the very set I'd brought home to the earl. One of the horseman, to be exact. Fashioned of that beautiful black ivory and fitted with a gold base. Do you recall how long I took in deciding what type of base should fit to each piece, Garn?"

"Aye. Too bloody long, m'lord," said Garn. He'd have smiled at the memory if not for the gravity and cruel, hideous reality of what had been that night's end. A dark light flitted through his gaze. "But I thought that chess set was . . . was lost among the ruins of your father's home, m'lord."

Julian nodded. "It was. Or *should* have been," he said. "I remember clearly placing it atop the sideboard that first night home, alongside all my father's other presents. Everyone else was in the front parlour. I remember because my mother . . . she—she had just redecorated the room and wished to have me make a toast to my father there. So I left the chess set on the board, boxed and wrapped and tied with that monstrous, ridiculous bow. Do you remember that bow, Garn?"

"Aye, m'lord, I be rememberin' it. You chose it because the earl would laugh at its gaudiness. And you, above all, wanted to see your father laugh that night because you'd been gone so long and missed him so terribly."

"Yes . . . yes, that's right," whispered Julian, now vividly caught up in replaying that night in his brain for what must surely be the millionth time, if not more. *"Gad,* Garn, but that chess set should have burned, melted, disintegrated, like everything else in that house . . . like *everyone* else."

Pain ripped a path through Julian's soul, as it always did when he thought of that grim August night.

Garn suddenly leaned forward. "Are you saying, m'lord, that whoever laid those explosives did so to get at the chess set?"

Julian got a grip on his emotions, took a deep breath, then said, "After tonight's revelations, Garn, it seems a likely possibility I shouldn't be ignoring. The diamond tucked inside one of those pieces was— *is*—worth a bloody fortune. Even more than the vast holdings of the Eve estates."

"The unholy bastard," Garn snarled, shifting his powerful arms atop the table and leaning forward even more. Darkly he whispered, "I swear to you, m'lord, if I ever find the person who did this, I'll gut him like the swine he is."

Julian believed him.

"There's more, Garn," he said. "The horseman in the packet . . . its base had been worked off, and a note was tucked inside, one demanding the Eve Diamond be revealed before the end of the Summer Season. There was no signature. No note of where to leave any information. 'Tis clear the person who took the set is now minus the diamond . . . and they must have reason to believe that whoever came for that package at Fountains knows where the diamond is."

"The woman?"

"No . . . I don't think so. I trailed her back to her rented rooms in Ripon and questioned her. She seemed truly clueless as to what the package held, but she did say she was retrieving it for a friend, some 'well-heeled lord' in London. That's why I'm here now, Garn. I'm going to go with her, back to Town, under the guise of her guard. She knows me only as Julian. Thinks I'm some kind of specter turned riverkeep, or some such rot. Whatever coil she's enmeshed herself in via this *friend* is, as we both know, a dangerous one."

Garn skewered him with a tight look. "Do you trust her, m'lord?"

The man's question took Julian by surprise. *Did* he trust Veronica?

"She could be leading you into a trap," Garn continued.

Ah, yes, Julian thought, *a perfect trap.*

But it wasn't the type of trap Garn was thinking—it was of a more physical kind. One of desire and need, one the lady could doubtless weave about him with her sheer beauty, innocent charm, and that reckless, ardent abandon she'd displayed beneath the onslaught of his kisses.

The very notion unsettled Julian more than he cared to admit. He yanked himself out of his reverie of Veronica's many enchantments.

"What I am certain of, Garn, is that she came to Fountains on an errand for another. And the packet she sought contained a piece of the gift I'd last given to my father. It's my belief that whoever sent her to Yorkshire most likely knows something about the blast that killed my family and left me without my hearing. I intend to trail her to London and enter into her circles. And intend to do all of this not as the seventh Earl of Eve, but as her hired guard."

Garn didn't even bat an eye at his lordship's wild plan. He simply nodded that understanding nod of his, and then asked, "How can I help, m'lord?"

Julian had known his manservant would react in such a way. He could forever and always count on Garn. There was no finer friend who walked the earth, Julian knew.

"I need you to go to London as well. I'll need a runner of information."

"Aye. I'll be that man, m'lord. Just tell me where and how."

"Go to my flat in St. James Place. My solicitor, Crandall, has a key. Tell Crandall I've returned to Town, get the funds you need from him. Tell him I'll contact him when I get to London. You wait for me at the flat. I will arrive there as soon as I can."

"Aye. Consider it done."

Julian nodded, realizing that he had no more time to spend in the cottage. He had a twenty-minute ride back to the village. And Veronica was waiting—or at least she'd better be.

"M'lord?" said Garn, as Julian made ready to leave. "You haven't told me the woman's name, or even where she resides."

"Her name is Veronica. Lady Veronica. That's all I know." He thought a minute, remembering how she had shuddered and turned away when he'd first touched her. Then he added, "No, there's one other thing I know about her. She's been abused, Garn. In some way, she's been hurt by someone."

Garn's blue eyes met Julian's black ones. *So the woman was a lady, no less, and had been hurt by some fiend.* The look in Garn's face registered those facts. He'd known a like lady at one time . . . had even married her, in fact, and laid her down in her grave, to boot.

Julian bade the man good-bye, then headed out of

the cottage to his mount. He angled his body up and on to the saddle, reined the stallion about, and then headed back to Ripon and the Cock and Dove Inn. Back to Veronica of the violet eyes, bewitching smile, soft curves . . . and the penchant to get out from under the thumb of her hired man.

God's teeth, but Julian was anxious to be near her again, to smell deeply of her rich, heady scent. Too, there was much he wished to learn about Veronica, about the soul inside of her, about why she'd feared he would strike her when they'd first met . . . and about why a lady such as herself seemed so eager to get away from her coachman.

Not even a full hour had passed since he'd seen her last. Odd, but it felt like a lifetime.

Julian was glad when his bay moved into an even faster lope.

Garn closed the door of the cottage once he'd seen his master and good friend had gotten safely on his way back to the village.

When he turned, he found Wil standing at the threshold beside the bedroom opposite Meg's.

"I heard voices," the young man said.

Garn sized up the youth, who'd grown tall as a post in what seemed to him an amazing short period of time. His eyes were green. Like Annie's. His mouth was wide and mobile, and this, too, Garn knew to have been bequeathed to him by the mother the boy had never known. His hair—a riot of golden reddish curls—was also reminiscent of the woman Garn had loved so fiercely and lost too soon.

But the young man's stance, his attitude, his temper, and his mistrust of the world at large, even his strong, finely muscled body, were wholly his father's.

And that, damn it all, was what Garn hated most—the father he now saw mirrored in the boy he'd tried to love but never quite could.

" 'Tis nothin' to worry yourself over, Wil. Go back to bed."

"It was the Earl of Eve who was here."

Garn hooked a look at him. "Aye, and so it was. What of it, boy?"

Wil defiantly shoved back a splay of curls spilling over his brow. "I thought he'd gone to Fountains to die," he said. "I thought you never expected to see him again."

Garn never minced words, and he did not do so now. "Aye," he said, nodding once. "I'd expected just that. But he's healed now and has no more need of those ruins."

"He's going back to London?"

"I think you know the answer to that, boy. I think, in fact, you heard everything."

A frown knit the young man's brow. "So you're going, too?"

"Aye. I'm going."

"And won't be returning here any time soon." It was a statement, not a question—and an accusatory one at that.

"I'll be back when I'm back," Garn said. "You're not to be leaving here and running away to London, as you did last August, you hear?"

"I didn't run away," Wil shot back. "I went there to see the father who has no time for me."

"The open road is no place for a boy alone, and you could have been killed in that explosion."

"But I wasn't," Wil snapped. "And if not for me, you'd have never found your way to his lordship in time to carry him out of that burning house. Because of me, he was saved from the flames."

Garn studied the young man. "Is there anything else you might have saved from those flames, boy?" he asked quietly.

Wil's green eyes narrowed. "You calling me a thief?"

"I'm asking you a question."

"If you had ever bothered to spend time with me, you wouldn't have to ask me anything. You'd know everything there was to know," he said and the animosity in his tone was unmistakable.

"Go on to bed, Wil. Think long and hard about whether there is something you wish to tell me," he said.

Garn leaned down to blow out the candle stub atop the table. Suddenly, the room was swallowed in darkness.

"Lately I've done nothing but think," said Wil, who turned back into his room and closed the door behind him.

Garn stood in the dark stillness, listening to the sounds of Annie's son moving away from him.

Nine

Veronica paced the confines of her rented chamber, her strides taking on a decidedly agitated tempo as she thought again of what Julian had proposed—no, *ordered*—her to do: accept him as her personal guard, inform her coachman he'd be returning to London with them, *and* leave a lamp lit for him. *Oh, but what devilish design could he possibly portend?*

Listening with irritation to the sounds of her abigail asleep and snoring softly in the connecting room, Veronica began to grow truly furious. Her personal guard indeed! Gad, that's exactly what she *did not* need. She had enough bother with the many watchdogs her father had overseeing her.

More to the point, however, was the fact that Julian's mere presence threw Veronica's emotions into a whirlwind. She had always kept her emotions tightly reined and her deepest feelings hidden, but this evening had proved to be the most emotionally charged one of her life—and all because of Julian. It was altogether too amazing to believe they'd actually met only a mere few hours ago. If this was what he could stir to life in her in such a short span of time, she could only imagine the outcome of having him near her day in and day out. The long journey back to London alone would doubtless find her a mass of quivering nerve ends, Veronica suspected.

For the life of her she could not puzzle out why Julian had so quickly jumped into her troubles concerning the packet. Certainly he'd met with some foul miscreants over the thing and been beaten soundly—but should not *that* have been incentive enough for him to want nothing further to do with her or the package? Why choose to get more deeply involved when he could simply not bother at all? And why, of all things, take the packet with him when it had been because of the blasted thing that he'd nearly been beaten to death? None of this made sense to Veronica.

As the minutes dragged past she became more and more agitated until, at last, there came a loud knock on the door.

Veronica whipped her attention to it like lead shooting from a gun barrel.

"Yes?" she called, thinking it was Julian, hoping it was Julian, then hoping it *wasn't* Julian, and all the while wondering whether or not she would open the door.

"I've made one last check on the cattle, m'lady. All is in ready to leave at dawn."

Shelton. Not Julian. For some absurd reason Veronica felt her heart sink a bit. Earlier, her coachman had dogged her way up the steps to her rented chambers, ascertaining for himself that she would indeed go straight to her rooms. Veronica had to admit she was glad, at once, for Shelton's shadow, for at that particular hour with all the revelers in the inn, and after having viewed Julian's beaten face, she'd been afraid to head up the stairs without company.

Thinking of all that, she replied, "Thank you, Shelton."

"So you are settled for the night, m'lady?"

Veronica knew that what her coachman was really inquiring was whether or not he could trust her to stay in her rooms and not go gadding off about the countryside.

"I am," she called back, wondering if the man would take it into his head to play sentinel at her door the whole night through.

She hoped not. If he did, he'd doubtless be rubbing elbows with Julian. The thought unsettled her further.

"Very well, m'lady. I'll be turning in for the night myself then."

He did not bid her a good night, nor she him. She heard the sounds of his heavy footfalls heading away; then she could hear nothing but the merriment from the lane outside and the taproom below.

And her maid's snores, of course. How the girl could so easily fall asleep, quick as a wink, was beyond Veronica.

When she'd informed Nettie they'd be leaving for London at dawn, the girl had immediately thrown herself into a frenzy of packing and preparing for the journey. Then she'd laid out her lady's traveling garments, plus night clothes and a light dressing gown. That done, she'd inquired, almost too eagerly, whether or not Veronica would be retiring any time soon.

"No," Veronica had said, adding that she could see to her own self this night. Then she'd hurried Nettie off to bed in the adjoining chamber, where the maid had promptly fallen asleep the moment, her brown-haired head pressed down atop the pillow.

Veronica had since decided only the truly innocent could sleep so soundly. She, herself, felt as though she were waiting to be taken to the guillotine.

And by none other than the dangerous stranger she'd unearthed from Fountains.

Veronica remembered again Julian's order for her

to leave a lamp lit for him. *Ha, in a pig's eye!* she decided vehemently.

In a fit of rebelliousness, Veronica doused the lamps of the chamber, casting herself into complete darkness. It appeared that the drapes covering the windows of the chamber were as thick as any tapestry that must have once adorned the inside walls of Fountains.

There, she thought, *that ought to serve him. He won't know which chamber is mine. He will bang about all the night, and with any luck I won't have to see him until morning.*

Feeling somewhat better, though not much, Veronica sat down on the huge bed, telling herself she would go to sleep and simply forget about the man she'd met at the abbey . . . forget about his kisses, his touch, and—

"Drat and blast," she said aloud into the thick darkness. Who was she trying to fool?

The mere memory of Julian's touches, the feel of his mouth on hers, was so firmly etched into her brain that she'd not be forgetting him at all.

There came a single sharp rap on the heavy oak door, the sound jerking Veronica from her thoughts.

" 'Tis me. Open the door."

Veronica did not need to be told the identity of the person now standing on the other side of the portal and rudely demanding entry.

She held perfectly still, hoping Julian would think that she was asleep or that he'd chosen the wrong room.

"I know you're not sleeping, Veronica. Now open this door. Unless, of course, you want me to rip it from its hinges."

Veronica's eyes widened. He wouldn't . . . would he? But she knew the answer.

"Devil take him," she muttered to herself, hastening to unlock the door before he thundered it apart, splinter by splinter.

He'd best have that dratted bundle with him, she thought because *that* was the *only* reason she was opening this portal. And when he stepped inside the room—if she was fast enough and wily enough—she would take the thing from his hands! And then . . . well . . . then she would simply scream for help.

It was a hopeless plan, Veronica knew, for what would she do when help *did* come running, only to find Lord Wrothram's youngest daughter alone in her rented rooms with a nefarious stranger?

All of these thoughts went winging through her mind as Veronica worked to get the door unlatched.

She'd no sooner pushed the bolt back than Julian pressed into the room, a spill of light from the hallway behind him throwing his entire body into one large, menacing shadow.

"I thought I asked that you leave a lamp lit," he groused.

Veronica could only gape at that black shadow that was his face.

"You didn't *ask* anything, sir," she reminded him. "You simply *ordered.*"

The difference seemed lost on him. "So why isn't one lit?" he demanded, stepping inside the chamber and swinging the door shut.

A huge darkness swallowed them, far deeper it seemed than the one Veronica had just sat amidst alone. Good Lord and good Lord. What was she doing, allowing this man into her rented bedchamber? She hadn't even spied the bundle in his hands. Maybe it was tucked in some pocket of his . . . maybe . . .

Veronica heard the too-final click of Julian throwing the bolt securely back into place. It sounded like a death knell. Notably, *hers.*

There came the briefest stirring of air against her. Veronica heard a soft muffle as his booted heel turned atop the wooden floor, accompanied by the whisper of his pant legs brushing together. He was turning to face her—a simple act, most assuredly, yet every movement of it seemed to be happening in slow, maddening motion, and all the while she wondered his intent—and even more so, she wondered what her reaction would be.

Would he touch her again, as he had at the abbey? Would he draw her close once more, so close that she'd be able to feel the deep, steady thud of his heart? *Did she want him to do so?*

"I-I'll light that lamp now," Veronica said, tamping down hard on her wanton thoughts.

"Don't bother. I'd wanted to see the light from the street only. Wanted to see what kind of a view anyone watching you would have. I'd intended to douse the thing the minute I got inside."

With that, he moved past her, only his shirtsleeve brushing lightly—and by sheer accident, it seemed—against her. He navigated his way to the curtained window, parting the heavy drape at one side with his forefinger and peering down at the busy street below. The light of the bonfires played fitfully over one half of his stony features, while the other half of his face remained claimed by the darkness of the room.

"Any visitors while I was gone?" he asked, not looking at her.

"Inside my bedchamber? Hardly," Veronica replied. "It seems there is only one brazen man about this night—you."

He ignored the rub. "Did you talk with anyone?" he demanded, his gaze continuing to search the sea of faces below.

How very rude of him to barge his way in here, bombard her with questions, and not even have the courtesy to look at her when speaking. "But of course I did," she snapped, her tone sounding childish even to her own ears. "All the king's horses and all the king's men. Not to mention—"

"Just answer the question," he cut in. "Did you *talk* to anyone, Veronica? Anyone at all?"

"No," she blasted, "no one other than my servants, not that it's any of *your* bloody business."

He finally looked at her, arching one brow at her churlish outburst. "If you don't quiet down, my lady, you'll wake that snoring maid of yours.

Veronica lifted her chin, defiant. Veronica knew that an uprising throughout the countryside wouldn't wake Nettie now that the girl had a full belly and a soft bed beneath her.

Veronica also knew she would not back down from this—this ruffian, and she would *not*, she told herself sternly, be aghast at her own uncivilized choice of words with him.

"Pray tell, just who do you think would be standing outside peering up at my window?" she demanded. "Other than the likes of you, that is."

"The likes of me? There you go again, Veronica, lumping me with every foul fiend who has ever walked this earth."

"And well I should! You've the stamp of a thorough beast!"

He said nothing for a full minute. Instead, he tested the window sash with one hand, seemed satisfied that it was secure, tested, too, the thickness of the heavy drapes, finding them satisfactory as well, then let the material fall back into place.

Darkness once again claimed the room.

"I suppose I deserved that," he finally said.

"Not to mention a great deal more," she muttered.

"I won't deny it, my lady."

"You—you have been insufferable this night, sir."

"Aye."

"And boorish and rude and—"

"Helpful. Don't forget helpful. With your injury to your . . . uh . . . leg, my lady," he roguishly reminded her.

Veronica's cheeks turned pink at the vivid memory of his roughened hands atop her thigh. "And then, to be even more alarmingly rude, you took the bundle. Where is it, by the way? Have you got it?"

"Ah, now the lady gets to the heart of the matter."

"Well? *Do* you have it?"

"Aye. I have it."

"With you? On your person?"

"No, my lady," he said, "but trust me when I say it is safe as a house. And that is about as much information as you'll be having from me on that score."

"But you'll retrieve it, in the morning, yes?"

"Yes. In the morning."

Veronica stood rooted to the spot where he'd left her by the door, her arms wrapped tight about her waist. She was feeling vulnerable and violated . . . and yet, heaven help her, there were tiny bursts of excitement bubbling up inside her at being closeted in this room, this darkness, with this man. The sound of his voice coming from across the chamber did odd things to her heartbeat, making it flutter, then pause, then beat a tattoo of thrills all the way from her head to her toes, over and over and over again.

"Feel free to light that lamp now, Veronica," he said. "Those drapes are as thick as any fog along the Thames. No one outside will be getting any kind of a view."

"Of all the— *You* light the blasted lamp!" Veronica exploded, mortified that while she'd been thinking of the man and the moment, he'd been contemplating the—the *drapes* of all things!

She thought she heard him chuckle softly, but she couldn't be certain, or the sound was smothered by his movements. She heard a further shuffle of sound and saw a spark that flared to a glow. Then the lamp's light blazed in the room, bouncing crazily for a moment and then settling to cast a soft light all about.

Veronica blinked against its vivid glow. The first thing she saw when her eyes adjusted to the brightness was Julian's gaze on hers, his one eye battered and salved and looking worse than she'd remembered.

He noted her attention to his face. "I am certain it appears far worse than it feels," he assured her.

Some of the fight washed out of Veronica and she felt truly ghastly that she'd just spoken so rudely to him.

"I . . . I am sorry you were attacked while retrieving the package, Julian."

He inclined his head to one side, curious and vigilant all at once. "Sorry enough to tell all about the bundle?"

"I-I told you. I came to Yorkshire to retrieve the package for a . . . a friend."

"Ah. Right. Some well-heeled lord in London. Care to share his name?"

Veronica shook her head. "I-I am not at liberty to say."

He frowned. "I thought as much." He drew in a breath, looked about the chamber, then nodded toward her maid's small, connecting room. "Is your abigail's window drawn?"

"Yes. Why do you ask?"

"Wouldn't want any late-night visitors trying to crawl through the thing."

"So you think the men who accosted you might possibly come looking for you?"

"Not me, Veronica. *You.* They came to find the person seeking the package. Unless there is some other young lady roaming Yorkshire on a mission for this 'friend' of yours, I suggest you'd best take an interest in protecting your own self."

Doubtless he was correct. Veronica shuddered once, then wrapped her arms more tightly about her waist.

"Feeling worried?" he queried. "Are you perhaps even beginning to question the merit of this 'friend' you seem so eager to protect?"

"No, not at all," Veronica replied, a shade too quickly, as she thought of Lord Rathbone. She reminded herself, however, that she'd come to Yorkshire solely for Pamela and *not* for Rathbone.

So thinking, she added, slowly and with more meaning, "I'll have you know I need not question this person's merit, sir. They are a good, true friend and would never lead me into danger."

As for where Rathbone would lead Pamela, that was another matter entirely, but Veronica dared not mention the man's name to Julian.

"Hmm," he merely murmured. "I hope you can claim the same once we reach London."

"Meaning?"

"Meaning, Veronica, a great many miles lie between here and there, not to mention long stretches of road where any rough sort could ambush your carriage. You would do well to make certain your coachman keeps his blunderbuss loaded and at the ready."

Veronica shifted nervously. "I-I do believe you are deliberately trying to frighten me."

"I do believe I am. You've a long way to travel with

a package that's already created quite a stir in just the span of an evening."

"Then I shall endeavour to be more careful."

"Rest assured, I am certain you shall, *because I will be with you every leg of your journey—and beyond.*"

"Oh." Veronica wrinkled her nose, not liking where the conversation was threading or how Julian was getting that look of portentous thunder on his brow. "You—you are no doubt referring to that—that outlandish notion of yours of becoming my personal guard."

"No doubt I am. And it is more than just a notion. It is now a reality."

"I am afraid it—it is out of the question, Julian," Veronica said, hoping a softer accent would help sway him. "I-I tried to tell you as much downstairs in the coffee room, but you did not seem inclined to listen."

"Nor am I so inclined to do so now," he stated.

"Be that as it may, my decision still stands. Though you might harbor some further sense of duty to me because of my predicament at Fountains and because I asked you to aid me in my mission, the simple truth of the matter is I have more than enough servants. Indeed, I feel I am constantly tripping over the lot of them, and well, you see, I . . . uh . . ."

Veronica stopped her spate of words, realizing with a sudden thud of embarrassment that Julian was barely listening to her ramblings. He had propped himself on a corner of the lamp table and folded his arms across his chest. He was, if she was not mistaken, contemplating not her words, but the full length of her body instead.

Veronica snapped her mouth shut tight as she felt that dark gaze of his move over every inch of her.

"I thought that might still your tongue," he said,

his voice low and turning husky. "Do you always talk so much, Veronica?"

She lifted her chin, unwilling to acknowledge how much his voice and his lingering gaze affected her. "You insult me, sir, both with your gaze and when you use my given name."

"You use mine," he said.

"Only because you . . . you insisted that I do so," she pointed out.

"You could have insisted otherwise." He watched her, quiet for a moment, then said, "The truth is, I enjoy saying your name. I like the way it feels on my tongue and moving past my lips."

Veronica experienced a whirling in her stomach with his words. Good Lord and good Lord. The man was the height of impropriety. And that look in his eyes, exuding a sexual prowess she'd had but a taste of at Fountains, warned her that she was playing with fire with this dangerous stranger.

"And your full name," he continued in that low, beguiling tone. "I am sure I would like that, too. What is it, my lady? Will you share it with me?"

Veronica took a deep breath, forcibly pulling herself out of the spell he was weaving about her with his voice and his gaze. Yes, she thought, she would inform him of her name and her father's and perhaps then he would not be so base as to address her like some rustic maid. In imperious accents, she said, "My full name, sir, is Lady Veronica Amelia Carstairs, and I am the youngest daughter of Earl Wrothram. My father is a very powerful and well-connected man in the elite circles of Society."

To Veronica's dismay Julian seemed unfazed by the information and only interested in her full given name. That dangerously seductive look in his eyes did not falter.

"You—you now know my full name, but you haven't yet given my yours," she said into the still quietness he seemed so comfortable to let hang between them.

"No I haven't, have I?" he finally murmured. He straightened away from the table, then began to move toward her. "Tell me, Lady Veronica Amelia Carstairs, do you plan to sleep standing upright and in full dress?"

So he intended to shock her, did he? She took a wary step back, glaring at him. "I'll probably not sleep at all, not that it is any of *your* affair."

He moved inexorably nearer.

"As your personal guard, Veronica, I should know these things. 'Tis a guard's duty to know if his lady is ready to flee at a moment's notice."

A few more steps and he'd be standing flush with her body.

Veronica scowled some more at him, then backed up all the way to the door.

"You—you are being thoroughly loathsome and vile and—"

"And just the sort of fellow you'll be needing if any thugs come calling for you or that bundle."

"You are truly mad if you believe I'm going to play along with your ridiculous game, sir."

" 'Tis Julian, Veronica. And of what game do you speak?"

He came to a stop, just a breath away from her.

Veronica forced herself not to tremble at his nearness. "This . . . this waggish train you've put into motion of being my guard of course," she managed to say.

"I find it a perfect plan, m'lady. I can protect you, can come between you and any raffish swine. I'll keep my eyes—or at least, one of them," he said, his bearded face creasing suddenly with that half smile of

his she was coming to know too well, "trained for any
signs of danger between here and London. All in all,
y'know, you ought to be thanking me for offering my
services as your personal guard. It's not every day I
lend myself to such a duty."

"Thanking you?" Veronica sputtered. "For such an
outrageous proposition? I think not, sir! What I *will*
be doing is reminding you I have not accepted those
services, not at all!"

"Ah, well, like it or not, you have them all the same.

"I don't like it. In fact, I only allowed you into this
chamber to tell you once and for all that I'll not be
having you as my personal guard or . . . or anything
of the sort."

That sloe-eyed smile of his deepened.

"And just *what* do you find so amusing?" she demanded hotly.

"We both know, Veronica, that the only reason you
opened that door is because you thought I'd come
walking in here with your package in my hands."

Veronica's cheeks flamed at the memory of her ill-
conceived plot to tear the thing out of his grip.

Seeing the telltale stain atop her cheeks, he said, "I
thought as much."

"Blast you," Veronica whispered, seething inside.

He stared at her for an uncomfortably long moment, his ravaged eye not nearly as frightening as the
other, which was smoldering to a deeper hue of black
as each second ticked past.

Languidly, he reached out, claiming hold of her, his
long, strong fingers splaying open about her elbows.
"There must," he whispered, moving his body closer
to hers, "be something of great worth in that bundle,
Veronica, to make you risk not only your safety in traveling to Fountains, but your reputation as well."

Veronica breathed in a sharp gasp and with it came

the heady, masculine scent of him. Gad, but she feared she might drown in that aroma, for it seemed to arrow directly into the deepest, most feminine part of her.

He was now standing too close. She could feel the heat of him, could feel his strength. Surely it was all a ploy on his part—a scheme to unsettle her, to make her tell everything, to confess all.

Veronica dug deep to find some composure. Lifting her chin, meeting his gaze with her own, she said staunchly, "I told you once and I'll tell you again, I don't *know* what the bundle contains."

His fingers kneaded the flesh beneath her muslin sleeves, coaxing goose pimples to flower atop her skin and down her spine, making her head feel woozy.

"Surely, Veronica," he murmured in that low, dreamy voice of his, "you've an inkling about its contents, about who might have ordered it to be placed at Fountains."

"No. I-I don't. *None.*"

"Ah, Veronica, do not say you simply dashed away from London, bringing an irate coachman with you, all the while in search of a packet, the contents and the origins of which you have no clue about."

"*Yes.* That—that is exactly what I am saying. I told you, I-I am on a mission. A Venus Mission. And what my duty entailed was to find the thing at Fountains and then take it back to—to . . ."

"Go on," he urged when she faltered. "You wished to take the package where? To whom?" He moved his hands farther up her arms, his fingers whispering softly over her sleeves and her skin beneath.

Oh, but he was playing a mesmerizing game with her!

"*To London,*" Veronica ground out, her words clipped as she yanked out of his hold.

Her violet eyes blazed as she stepped to the side and

away from him, cornering herself by the head of the bed and the latch of the door.

"That is the story, sir. That is all I know, and it is *all* you'll be hearing from me. And now," she said, reaching a shaking hand behind her for the bolt of the door, "I suggest you take your leave, sir."

To her consternation, Julian did not budge.

"Are you going to wait until I scream for help?" she asked.

He shook his head. "You won't be screaming, Veronica."

"And how can you be so certain?"

"Because there is something about your Venus Mission you are not telling me. And that something, my lady, will keep you quiet. Of that much, I am certain."

Veronica wanted to thrust him out the door and slam the thing behind him.

But she didn't. She couldn't.

He was, alas, correct.

"I want you to leave," she said again, ignoring the hammering of her own heart.

"And why is that, Veronica? Because I make you nervous with my questions? Or with my presence?"

Both! she wanted to shout.

"Neither," she said, with all the dignity she could muster. And then, a thought striking her, she added, "Since you are so eager to serve as my personal guard, sir, it would bode well for you to know that all those in my service do exactly as I deign."

His black gaze gleamed. "Is this your way of informing me, my lady, that you are a hard taskmistress?"

Veronica nodded, finally feeling as if she had some ground to stand on with this man. "My servants do what I demand, when I demand it," she said in a perfect lie. "If—if you are to be my personal guard, sir, you must do as I say, *only* as I say."

The light in his eyes turned smoky. "Ah, so I am to be my lady's slave." His gaze moved from her eyes to her mouth. "It does not sound like such a horrible existence," he murmured huskily.

Veronica felt a wave of heat wash through her. The meaning of his words and the train of his gaze was not lost on her. He was, in his own graceless and shocking fashion, reminding her of the kisses they'd shared at the abbey, of their touches, too. Drat him, but he'd rounded the tables on her once again, manipulating not only the moment, but her emotions as well.

Veronica decided it best to act as though she did not read the real meaning of his words. Far better to just end this conversation and do so quickly, she thought, and said, "I-I am glad we have come to an understanding." She opened the door wide, motioning him out into the hall. "Good night, sir."

" 'Tis Julian," he rakishly reminded her again.

The last thing Veronica saw as she pushed the door shut was that too-handsome grin upon his bruised and battered face.

Ten

Julian spent a long night outside of Veronica's door. He dozed off in short spurts and was disturbed by someone only once, about four in the morning. It proved to be one of the inn's maids, a little bosky but not fully top-heavy from her night of celebrating Midsummer's Eve. She'd come upstairs to douse the lamps she should have seen to hours ago.

Julian helped her with the task and then, at her insistence, was bequeathed a mighty feast for his troubles. The maid brought up a platter of meats and cheeses, hunks of bread, and even a draught of milk for him.

"Thank you," Julian said with a smile.

"It be no trouble," the maid replied, "and I'll not even be askin' why yer sleepin' outside her ladyship's room. I won't ev'n let on to the innkeep 'bout it."

Julian reached deep into his pocket to give her some kind of payment, but found only a sixpence, a shilling, and a few half crowns. He frowned, remembering that he'd left his purse, along with Veronica's package, with his mount. All were being well protected by a stable hand Julian had met years ago in Ripon—a man who knew only that Julian was a friend of Garn's and was quite an accomplished boxer, a man whom Julian knew he could trust.

He gave the maid the coins. The girl seemed to

think it a windfall. She beamed him a pretty smile and then left him in the hallway.

Julian ate every bit of the food, then settled against Veronica's door, hearing the creak of that huge bed of hers as she shifted her position. He tried not to imagine the sight of her in nothing but a night rail, her lustrous hair fanned out atop her pillow, that kissable mouth of hers opened slightly as she slumbered. The image, however, presented itself all too clearly in his mind.

Julian leaned his head back against the door, forcing himself instead to study the small patch of pre-dawn sky visible through the smudged window of the hallway.

This day marked a new beginning for him. He was headed for London. At long, long last, he was going to make some headway into learning who'd murdered his family . . . and Lady Veronica would be the one to lead him on that trail.

Julian frowned as he thought of the moments with her in the rented chamber. His behavior had been inexcusable, he knew. He'd been boorish and base, his conduct anything but that of a gentleman. He'd been deliberately roguish, knowing full well she was affected by him, and hoping to take advantage of that weakness. But when he'd touched her he'd realized he was just as affected by their nearness and he'd had to fight down the urge to gather Veronica into his arms and kiss her as he had done at Fountains.

He had no excuse for his behavior other than he wished to ferret out the murderer of his beloved family. Finding the culprit was the only thing that mattered to him. The only thing that *could* matter. He'd thought to coax truths from the lovely Veronica, but had learned only what he'd already deduced earlier in the evening: that she truly did not know about the contents of the bundle. She was an innocent party in the mystery. Her "friend" in London, however, was not.

At sight of the sky at last lightning through the dirty window, Julian got to his feet and gave a knock on Veronica's door. " 'Tis morning, my lady, and time to leave."

"I am awake," she called, and by the sound of her voice had been awake for a good long while.

So, they'd both had a sleepless night, Julian thought to himself, and he wondered what thoughts had been tumbling through her mind. He'd given her every reason to loathe him—a fact that left a very ugly taste in his mouth. No doubt she'd spent the night fretting over what ill-mannered liberties he might try to take during their travels to London and fearing, too, whether or not he would have a loose tongue concerning their indiscretion at Fountains.

Julian made a mental note to be on his best behavior where Veronica was concerned. She was a lady, not some hardened wanton, and he would treat her as such, despite the intimacies they'd shared.

He waited a moment longer, hearing the muffled sounds of her movements in the room and then the sleepy voice of her maid. After checking the landing and assuring himself all was quiet on this floor and that Veronica would not be set upon the minute she walked out of her door, Julian headed downstairs.

The taproom, with its smoke-blackened beams, was empty save for one bedraggled man sleeping off a night of drunkenness. The coffee room was also quiet, its door standing ajar. Julian moved into the kitchen, where a blear-eyed cook, and the maid he'd met earlier, had roused themselves and were setting to the task of preparing breakfast.

The maid brightened at sight of Julian and, ignoring the cook's curious stare, hurried toward him. "Wud ye be wantin' some porridge or toast, sir?" she asked.

Julian shook his head. "No, thank you. But might there be a room where I can freshen up? I've a long day of travel ahead and—"

"Say no more, sir," the maid cut in, smiling that pretty smile of hers, and before the cook could stop her she led Julian out of the kitchen, then through a maze of narrow corridors to a small room at the very ends of the inn.

"Ye just 'elp yerself, sir," she said, popping the door open. The room was small and crudely furnished, but clean. "Now don't be thinkin' I let just anyone in 'ere. I don't. But ye 'ave been generous w' yer coin so I be generous in like. There be a basin of fresh wat'r and— and I not be mindin' at all if'n ye be usin' me comb and some of me ribbon fer that handsome 'ead of 'air of yers."

Julian ran one hand through the shagged lengths of his black locks. "Ribbon, you say?"

"Aye. Red and blue, ev'n pink," she said proudly, then left him alone, hurrying back to her duties.

Julian decided at that moment that once he'd reached London and his solicitor he would make certain the young maid was forwarded a tidy sum for her kindness. He moved toward the basin that sat atop a small, rickety washstand and commenced to wash away the stains of Fountains and his beating. Above the basin, hung at a crooked angle, was a cracked looking glass, smoked by age.

Julian chanced a glance at his reflection, startled by what he saw. Zounds, but he appeared leaner, harder, edgier than he ever had in his life. His time at the abbey had taken its toll, casting his features into sharp, harsh lines, as though they'd been fash-

ioned from the hardest flint. And the beating he'd
taken at the hands of the ruffians had left its stamp
as well. There were bruises along his strong, broad
cheekbones, the cut on his lip had swelled to an angry slash of tender-looking pink, and his right eye . . .
bloody hell but the thing, though salved, had swollen
grotesquely and was now a nasty shade of bluish-
black tinged with purple. No wonder Veronica's
abigail had drawn back in horror when he'd stepped
into the coffee room last night. Julian grimaced at
the memory.

But Veronica. Ah, the brave, beautiful Veronica had
met him stare for bleary-eyed stare and had not
swooned at the spectacle he presented, but had instead pushed him down atop a chair and taken it upon
herself to minister to his injuries.

And now, this morning, she was going to face her
devil of a coachman and somehow explain why Julian
would be returning with them to London.

Julian frowned at his own reflection at that thought.
He'd given her no quarter but to accept him as her
guard, and she'd finally acquiesced—but at what cost
to her own self he now wondered.

Julian suspected there was something not quite
right within Earl Wrothram's household. No genteel
lady should be so frightened of a mere coachman her
father employed. But fear the man Veronica did. *Why?*
he wondered.

And why, Julian further pondered, would Veronica
allow Julian his head, accept him to play her guard,
when in doing so she would doubtless lay herself prey
to her coachman's ire.

The only answer could be that, whoever this friend
in Town of hers was, the person held great sway over
her. Clearly Veronica would risk a great deal for this
"friend." The mere thought that this person could be

Veronica's intended or mayhap even her lover left an ugly, hideous taste in Julian's mouth. He did not like at all the possibility of Veronica having known—and liked—another man's touch or kiss. And that the very lovely lady might have set her heart on a swell who had not the backbone to retrieve his own bloody package made Julian's blood boil. As for the fact this swell might have the Eve Diamond, might have been the one to plant the explosives and kill his family . . . ah, that made Julian's entire being convulse with rage.

With all these thoughts banging through his mind, Julian scowled at his battered reflection, then leaned low over the basin and set in earnest to the task of washing his face and neck and hands with the crude bar of soap that sat beside the basin.

A short time later, his ablutions nearly finished, Julian combed the tangles from his hair and tamed the urge to just shear the locks. Only when the murderer of his family was revealed would he shave and cut his hair. Until then, he'd go about like some mad Byron, his locks long.

Spying the maid's ribbons, Julian reached for one— the red one. He pulled his long hair back and tied it into a queue with the ribbon, its ends trailing to his broad shoulders.

He glanced once again at his reflection, deciding he looked like a damned pirate of old and certainly not what he truly was—the seventh Earl of Eve. 'Twould have to do, though, and his act of cleaning up a bit would have to be enough so that he did not appear a total ruffian in the sight of Veronica's servants. She would have a difficult enough time of it in explaining his presence, let alone in seeing that he was accepted as her guard.

Julian frowned, his battered eye looking even more grim in the looking glass as he did so. If that brute of a coachman made one untoward comment to Veronica, Julian would lay the man low with the mightiest of boxing punches, he vowed silently to himself.

His mood darkening, Julian left the room, deciding he'd best have a word with the lady's coachman before he was forced into fisticuffs with the man.

Julian found Shelton in the kitchen seeing that Veronica's breakfast was being prepared. The minute Julian entered the room the coachman stiffened, glowering at him.

"Not you again," he muttered.

"Aye. 'Tis me, and I'd like a word with you."

Shelton waved one arm at Julian, dismissing him. "I've no time for your like. Begone," he said in a warning tone, heading out the back door of the kitchen and no doubt intending to see to the cattle and Veronica's carriage.

Julian doggedly followed him.

They got as far as the water pump before the huge, hulking coachman whirled about, hitching up his coat sleeves as he did so. "You want trouble, man?" he asked, his deep baritone voice disturbing the few chickens that pecked at some feed on the ground near the well. "Then so be it. I'll give you trouble—enough to make sure you'll not be bothering my lady again."

Julian spread his arms wide. "I simply wish to talk with you. Set you clear on a few things."

"And what might *that* be, you lowly sewer rat? Eh? I've seen your kind. Aye. Know it well, in fact. Looking for an easy way . . . mayhap even an easier lay."

"God's teeth," breathed Julian, "but you should mind that tongue of yours."

"Pah," Shelton spat. "I saw how my lady reacted to you last night. Don't think I don't know she went to those gawdforsaken ruins to meet with you, to be alone with you and do things she ought not be doing.

But there you erred, man. You see, Earl Wrothram, he knows that his youngest daughter is the spittin' image of her mother. A lightskirt's daughter, that's what the young gel is—a seed from one of her mother's many indiscretions—and destined to repeat her mother's sordid past. That's why I'm paid heavily to follow her every footstep, make sure she doesn't share her charms with every fool who looks her way." Shelton curled his lip at Julian. "Appears I came too late this time, eh? No doubt she let you have a taste of her charms at that abbey."

Julian suddenly felt his insides burn with hideous anger. So *this* was the reason the too-sweet and innocent Veronica had said she had too many servants watching over her . . . and doubtless here was the reason she'd pulled back when he'd first reached out to touch her after he'd catapulted them over that ledge at Fountains . . . because she'd feared he would strike her. Could the lady's father, and mayhap even this brutish coachman, have struck her during her young life? Could they have done so more than once?

"B'God," Julian rasped, hoping against hope that wasn't the way of it. "The lady is an innocent, undeserving of such rotted talk."

"Yeah, yeah," breathed Shelton, clearly not agreeing, "and King George is as sane as you, eh, you sewer rat?"

Julian did not pause to think twice. With a savage growl he charged at the coachman, slamming against the man's mighty girth, knocking into his midsection with one shoulder and thrusting him back and down.

Shelton's huge body hit the earth with a thud. The chickens squawked, feathers ruffling as they darted away to safety.

Shelton let forth a grunt of surprise. "What the—"

Julian grabbed the brute by the scruff of his collar,

yanked his bull-like head up, and said, in no uncertain terms, "Hear me and hear me well, you piece of hired vermin. The young woman you've been paid to watchdog is a lady in the truest sense of the word. She is no more a woman of sullied morals than you are a man of distinction. She *did not* go to Fountains to meet me, you ass, but did so as a favor to a friend. And I no more had my way with her than any other man has. She is pure, do hear? *Pure and sweet and all that is good,* and a damned sight better than you or her father obviously are."

Julian was past reason. He knew only a furious rage buffeting through him. It seemed that his exile at Fountains had brought out the very beast in him, that no longer was he the Earl of Eve, but rather a creature of animalistic instincts, something akin and not very much above the wild dogs that roamed the abbey's ruins.

He pressed his large hand about the man's meaty throat, tightening his hold. "You will *not* be informing Earl Wrothram of Lady Veronica's sojourn to this shire, sir, nor," he added, his voice a grim note, his body bearing down hard on the man's, "will you be denying the fact that I have now chosen to be your lady's personal guard."

Shelton's eyes went wide at that last bit of news as he tried to throw Julian off of him. But Julian held tight, bearing down with even more force.

"Aye," Julian muttered, purposefully lowering his lips toward the coachman's face, so that the man could make no mistake of hearing him fully. "I am taking it upon myself to accompany your lady and you back to London. My sole task is to guard her ladyship. And trust me, I am not a man to be thwarted. Give your lady any trouble and you'll have me to deal with. Alert her father about her journey to the abbey and you'll face the same. Do I make myself clear?"

The coachman glared up at him. "You're crazed, man."

"Aye. I am, and you don't know the half of it—not by far—so do not cross me."

The man shifted a bit, weighing all he'd just learned, and then, suddenly, his anger at being shoved to the ground seemed to dissolve. He went slack beneath Julian.

"What's this . . . some trick on your part, you vile piece of vermin?" Julian breathed.

"No, no tricks. I am not going to spar with you, man. And you have my word, whoever you are, that I'll not be telling Earl Wrothram about his daughter's journey here. 'Tis clear as bells you care about the lady—God knows she needs someone to be caring about her."

Julian cocked one brow at the coachman's change of mood.

"Naw, don't be glaring at me with that banged-up, suspicious eye of yours. I'm trying to tell you I'm ready to hear you out, man. Now why don't you get that ugly mug of yours out of my face and let me stand upright?"

Julian, still not fully trusting the brute, but realizing there was a definite change in the wind, slowly got to his feet, even reaching down to give the coachman a hand.

The man accepted the offer, stood up, then brushed off the seat of his pants. Julian was surprised when the coachman offered a handshake.

"The name's Shelton," he said. "Since you're so hell-bent on being the lady's guard, I s'pose we ought to introduce ourselves."

Julian warily took the man's hand and shook it. "Julian," he replied.

"I won't be asking how you got that swollen face, Julian, but you're obviously able to hold your own. So glad I am you'll be joining us for the ride back to London. Come on," he said, releasing his hold on Julian's hand. "We can talk while we head to the stables."

Julian sized up the man, unable to trust the change in him.

"Are you coming or not?" Shelton grumbled in a gruff tone that sounded surprisingly friendly.

"Coming to be sure, but I must say I am surprised at the change in your manner."

"I'm not so terrible, though I've been paid to be a frightening presence to Earl Wrothram's daughters. Was told to keep them under thumb and didn't have much say in the matter." He started walking.

Julian followed.

"I'll tell you this much," Shelton continued. "I haven't had an easy time of it since Lady Veronica came to Town with her sister. She's always sneaking out of her father's house, she is, running hither and yon 'bout London, and her father yelling to me that he doesn't trust her. I had no choice but to follow her, to be gruff with her. But in my heart of hearts, truth be known, I never did believe the young lady was up to no good. And I never could understand why she wasn't claimed right fast by some swell and swept toward the altar."

"So why hasn't she—been led to the altar, that is?" Julian asked.

Shelton shrugged his huge shoulders. "Can't say. The lady doesn't exactly confide in me, o' course. I got an opinion, though."

"And that is?"

"I think she's decided never to marry. To be independent. No doubt it's because she's known the heavy hand of her father and wishes naught to spend her adult life as she has her childhood."

"And how was her childhood?" Julian asked, almost afraid to hear the answer.

"Rough, I gather. She was but ten when her mother died, though I can't say as though Countess Wrothram was probably ever one to be mothering any child. Had a liking for laudanum, and before that for any man other than the earl."

"Good God," Julian breathed.

"Now Lady Veronica's father," Shelton went on, clearly glad to finally be sharing his thoughts with someone, "he seems to think the reason she's taken no marriage offers is because she's sullied herself with more than one man. But me, I never could be believing such a thing, though there were times—such as when I found her at the abbey—that I had to take pause and wonder."

They were now nearing the stables.

"I've always believed in the lady's innocence," Shelton continued, "but her father's suspicions and cruel treatment of her made me think I was wanting to see something in her that wasn't there. And . . . and of course," Shelton added, almost guiltily, "the man pays me a heavy bit to dog his daughter's every step."

Julian let out a grunt of disgust. "The man must be a devil."

"Aye, there are those in Society what call him that. Just between us, his bad temperament has been fueled by his dead wife's wantonness those many years past. Once she'd tamed her wildness, the countess spent her last days in her chambers, taking no visitors other than her physician, since he kept her supplied with her drug. Lady Veronica and her sister never had much love from their parents. The earl moved to London the day his wife was laid to rest. Left his daughters in the care of some aged governess.

"He was glad enough to keep them tucked away at one of his country estates. Only when they reached a marrying age did he bring the gels to London. His oldest daughter, Lady Lily, she made quite a splash her first time out, got some offers, too, but only from rakes looking to line their pockets. The earl turned them all away. But Lady Veronica, ah, now she made an even bigger splash, had some fine offers, too. Earl Wrothram, though, he nipped 'em all in the bud. Said she'd not be marrying until he decided and she seemed none too eager to gainsay him, though there was one young buck she might have taken a shine to."

"Who?" Julian heard himself ask, with a little too much interest.

Shelton thought for a minute, then frowned. "Can't recall his name. Some blond fellow, rather tame. Not too high in the instep. She seemed to like his gentleness, but after a heated argument with her father, she ignored even him."

Julian stared straight ahead, his gut clenching. Could this be the person for whom she'd come to Yorkshire on a mission? Did she love him? Had she ever shared a kiss with him? Was she even now eager to return to Town to see him, to deliver to him in private the package she'd been so set on finding?

Julian brought his mind back to the present. Shelton was still talking. ". . . and because the earl took himself off to Bath for a few weeks is the only reason Lady Veronica dared to come to Yorkshire. She'd never have managed such a scheme had her father been in residence."

Julian blinked, trying to catch up with the conversation. "So Lord Wrothram is that beastly to his daughter?"

"Aye," Shelton replied. "But not nearly as brutal as he used to be, when she was but a young girl—or so I've been told. Like I said, she hasn't always lived in London with him. Lady Wrothram, in the past, was wont to travel from one holding to the other, never finding one to her he liking, but she finally settled down in Devonshire one year, and stayed there until she died. Lady Veronica and her sister reluctantly came to London little more than a year and a half ago for Lady Lily's come-out."

"And Lady Veronica?" Julian asked. "When was her first Season?"

"Just this past spring, though she'd as like have rather gone to the devil and supped with him instead, I s'pose. She hates Town life, I believe . . . or mayhap it's just being under his lordship's tight rule that she hates."

"I shouldn't wonder why," groused Julian. He came to a halt just before they crossed the lane to the stables. "Can I take it," he asked, "that the two of us might be able to endeavour to protect the lady we've both come to admire and care about? Though you've been doing her father's bidding, Shelton, I see in you a hankering to protect and believe in her. Am I right?"

Shelton reached up with one meaty fist to tug his collar from his neck. "Aye," he said, with meaning in his tone, "though I've played the devil's advocate with Lady Veronica for far too long, you are right about that. I *do* care about her. And I do think that, no matter what else she discovered at Fountains, she found a true friend in you. And it is a true and honest friend she'll be needing should the earl ever learn of her sojourn here—though he'll not be hearing it from these lips."

Julian nodded at the man. "Glad I am to hear you say that, Shelton." He motioned toward the stable yards, where several hostlers and postilions made quick work of hitching the many cattle into the traces of various kinds of rigs and chariots. "Shall we go? We've a long way before we reach London."

"Aye, too many miles," Shelton said. "But you'll no doubt be impressed with her ladyship's carriage. Smart and fleet it is, designed to have four cattle at its head. The road back to London won't be so long, given the carriage's light weight and the prime cattle we'll hitch to it along the way. Earl Wrothram spares no expense—not even for the daughter he thinks is a lightskirt."

Julian winced at that last remark, but followed Shelton nonetheless. They'd come to an understanding, he and this brute of a coachman. Julian was glad.

Far better it would be to ride the Great North Road back to the heart of London with Shelton as his ally instead of his enemy. With the coachman's blunderbuss and brawn, and with Julian's dogged determination and fearlessness, they might actually see Veronica delivered safely back home—and directly into the arms of the "friend" she was reluctant to name . . . a person who might even be the one man Veronica had thought to marry.

Less than an hour later, Julian watched as Veronica, garbed in a travelling dress of the prettiest lilac, and accompanied by her abigail, made her way toward the smart carriage with its team of four. The carriage's colors of maroon and gold flamed in the early morning light.

Julian sat astride his own mettlesome mount, the beast showing eager signs to be on the open road.

"Good morning, my lady," Julian said to Veronica, wishing now that he had a proper hat atop his head so that he could tip it her way in gentlemanly fashion. But alas he was clothed in his threadbare shirt and breeches, scuffed boot, and little else. With no hat to tip, he leaned slightly forward at the waist, hoping to convey to her with that small gesture that he'd not be acting like the lowly beast she must think him to be. As he did so, the ends of the ribbon he'd been bequeathed by the inn's maid lifted slightly with the breeze, playing atop each of his broad shoulders.

Veronica glanced up at Julian from beneath the wide brim of her straw hat, trimmed around the crown with flouncy ostrich plumes. If she was surprised by the pricey horseflesh he sat atop, she made no show of it. Julian caught a glimpse of those stunning violet eyes of hers, saw the way her kissable mouth pursed briefly as she contemplated how much or how little he might be saying in front of her servants, and then, with a quick answering nod toward him, looked away.

"Lawks, m'lady," Julian heard the abigail exclaim, "d'not say 'at dang'rous strang'r frum last night be joinin' us on our jo'rney 'ome!"

"Very well," he heard Veronica reply. "I'll not be saying it, Nettie. Now do climb inside while I speak with Shelton."

The maid cast a wide-eyed glance up at Julian, then scurried to climb the iron steps Shelton had let down from the carriage.

Veronica looked at her coachman, lifting her chin in what could only be a brave bit of daring. "I-I have hired this man to be our guard during our journey home, Shelton. Given all that could beset us over the many miles back to Town, I-I thought it would be best."

"Very good, my lady," Shelton replied, doing his best to maintain a stony face.

Julian noted Veronica's brief hesitation at her coachman's docile attitude. Carefully, she added,

"I . . . I may even keep the man in my employ once we reach London, Shelton."

For good measure the coachman appeared as though he would protest mightily and question her decision, but then nodded, and said simply, "Aye, my lady. As you see fit."

Veronica cast the man a quizzical glance, clearly surprised by his response. She'd doubtless expected him to give her a difficult time and to prove to be a brick wall.

Shelton merely stood still, awaiting the moment when she climbed into the carriage. Veronica, casting another glance at Julian from beneath the brim of her bonnet, did just that.

Shelton lifted the steps back into place, shut the door, then moved to climb atop his box, taking up his whip as he did so.

In the next moment, the coachman urged the horses into motion, and the smart carriage sprang forward, away from the Cock and Dove Inn and heading south to London, Julian riding at a brisk pace behind.

Eleven

A fuming Veronica sat stiffly atop the rich leather squabs inside her carriage, staring straight ahead and feeling absolutely furious. After a long, restless night of fretting about how she would approach with Shelton the subject of Julian being her guard, and equally long hours and reflecting about her wanton thoughts and reactions whenever she was in the Julian's presence, what should she come out of the inn to find? Her coachman acting like some docile bit of mash . . . and Julian—*oh, Julian*—astride some fancy bloodstock that could only have been purchased at Tattersall's (or stolen from some swell who *had* purchased the beast there) looking smug and as cleaned up as a shiny new penny!

To think she'd wasted an entire night of sleep fussing about the man, wondering if he was comfortable outside her door, wondering if he'd be set upon by those thugs again while keeping watch over her, worrying about his hearing and if the beating he'd taken could have caused him serious damage, worrying about his eye and if he'd be able to see clearly once the swelling went down . . . and—and thinking, *blast it all,* about every breath she could hear him draw at the other side of her door.

Clearly she shouldn't have bothered to worry one

second over his welfare. He seemed to have fared perfectly well on his own!

Did the man have to appear so blasted refreshed this morning, as though he'd slept the sleep of the innocent and not the damned, and had just partaken of a king's feast? He'd somehow managed to tear himself away from the ridiculous business of being her personal guard long enough to clean himself up. And that ribbon in his hair—*where on earth* had he managed to procure *that*? she wondered, angry at herself for thinking him far too handsome with his black locks pulled back, one lone wave falling rakishly over his battered eye. And drat her own traitorous body for responding to the sight of him like some lovesick chit!

"He be ev'r so 'andsome," said Nettie, as though reading her lady's thoughts and nodding in perfect agreement.

"What? *Who?*" Veronica demanded.

"The man whut you found to guard us back to Town, o' course. Coo, m'lady, where'v'r did y' find 'im?"

Beneath a rock, Veronica wanted to say, *and I welcome him to climb back under it!*

Nettie, however, did not wait for her lady to answer; her attention was now focused on the window—or rather, the person she could see through the small pane.

"La, m'lady, look! Yer guard, 'e be ridin' fer the road in front of us, no doubt t' check fer 'ighwaymen and the like." Nettie let out a sigh of wondrous rapture, thoroughly enchanted. "Not only 'andsome but brave, too. Stop me, m'lady, but y' sh'ld be 'irin' all the servants, I vow, if this be proof of yer fine taste in such matters."

"Really, Nettie. That is quite enough."

The abigail wasn't listening. In a rash heat of excitement, the girl let down the window, then stuck her head fully out, her poke bonnet banging against the top side of it as she did so. "Lawks, sir," she called to Julian, no doubt sending him a silly, moon-eyed smile. "I never be seein' such a fine mount, I swears! Howev'r did y' come by it?"

Julian leaned down, running one large and gloved hand over his horse's sleek black neck. " 'Twas a gift, mistress," he said, sending the maid a jaunty smile. He met Veronica's furious gaze over the girl's bonnet, then added, "A gift from a friend . . . one who did not even expect me to, say, perform a mission for it."

"Oh, coo," breathed Nettie, clearly enthralled, "we sh'ld all 'ave such fine friends, sir."

"Yes," agreed Julian. "We should indeed." And again, his darkling gaze met with Veronica's.

His meaning was not lost on her.

"That's enough, Nettie," Veronica snapped. "Do get your body back in here, sit down, and—and behave yourself. I'll not have you hanging yourself out the window, ogling the man, or even talking to him. 'Tis unseemly."

"Yes, m'lady," said Nettie, chastened. She slid once again down onto the seat, plopped her body back against the squabs and remained sullenly quiet.

But Nettie was correct. Julian's mount was indeed a pricey one and not at all in keeping with what one would expect of a lowly riverkeep who dwelled in the prisons of some ruinous abbey. Had he stolen the animal, expensive saddle and all—plus the fine gloves he was now wearing? Was this dangerous stranger a thief of the highest order?

It did not bear thinking of all Julian could be or have done; the possibilities were endless and Veronica had known that fact from the first moment she'd met him.

No, what bothered her most at the moment was that Julian had somehow managed to worm his way into the good graces of her coachman. That Nettie had taken a quick shine to him was not so remarkable. The girl's head would turn at any handsome face, no matter how bruised and cut. But Shelton, he was much more worldly wise than her fanciful abigail, which left Veronica with only one conclusion. The two of them had doubtless met up at some point between darkness and dawn, and had come to some sort of an agreement.

Could Shelton have struck a bargain with Julian, cajoling him with promises of heavy payment to go before her father and tell all of what had happened at Fountains?

Veronica's blood went cold at the possibility. What her father would do, if he ever learned of her sojourn north, she didn't even dare consider. His cruelty to her during her youth would probably pale in comparison. . . .

Veronica vowed to herself that before they reached London she would have a strong word alone with Julian.

It was at Grantham, *finally,* that Veronica, dressed in her riding habit, hired a hack and determined to ride to the next stage at Stamford alongside Julian. She was not surprised when Shelton allowed her her head in this decision.

An audience with the Prince Regent would doubtless have been easier to orchestrate than a private moment with Julian during this journey back to London. Over the many miles they'd traveled since Ripon and the many stages they'd paused at, Julian had thoroughly charmed her abigail and appeared to have won over the prickly Shelton. With a grace that seemed to come easily to him he had won the undying respect of every innkeep, ostler, serving maid, and chambermaid with whom they came in contact. His growing popularity incensed Veronica no small amount.

She urged her rented saddle horse into motion, hurrying to catch up.

"You might consider slowing your pace," she called to Julian. "I am trying to have a word with you—and *have been* since we left Ripon."

Julian glanced back, slowing his beast to an easy stride at sight of her. "My lady," he said, inclining his head slightly in greeting, even tipping the low-crowned hat he'd somehow procured during their travels. The thing was of dubious origin, brown in color, and sported a single fresh rose, probably passed to him by some admiring young maid. "If you wished to speak with me, my lady, all you had to do was say so. As I recall from our conversation at the Cock and Dove, I am to do as you demand whenever you deign . . . something akin to a—what was it? Ah, yes, a slave."

Rude of him to remind her—and blast it, the idea of his being her slave had been *his,* not hers.

"Oh?" Veronica replied instead, sounding churlish even to her own ears. "And when, pray, have you even offered me that chance? It appears you've been far too busy with all your admirers along the road. And by the bye, whatever were you doing outside the private parlour while I dined last evening?"

"Curious? You could have opened the door and found out."

Veronica sent him a withering look.

Julian laughed. "Ah, my lady is in no mood for guessing, no? Very well, I'll tell. The boot boy came along. He had some dice in his pocket and time on his hands, so he challenged me to a few rolls; if he lost I'd get my boots shined, free of charge." He glanced at the road ahead of them.

"And?" Veronica demanded when Julian seemed done with talking.

He nodded toward his newly polished boots. "And I'd say he did a bang-up job."

Veronica was in no mood to play at small talk or endure Julian's newfound good humor.

Eyes narrowing, she said, "You appear to have planked the gap with my coachman. Do you care to explain that, sir?"

"What's to explain?" he asked with a shrug of his broad shoulders. "I simply informed the fellow I'd be your guard during the journey back to London. Given the fact you raced north to Yorkshire with no footman, I s'pose the chap was glad enough to have another man along for the ride."

"I find that difficult to believe. Shelton's ego concerning his ability to watch over anyone aboard the carriage he drives knows no bounds. No, it is quite clear to me the two of you have some train in motion and are quite possibly in cahoots."

"Surely you are imagining things."

"I think not," Veronica insisted. "The two of you appear as thick as thieves, even taking your meals together and—"

"Would you rather I took my meals with *you?*" Julian asked, a ghost of a grin playing on his lips—a grin very much like the one he'd given her that night at the Cock and Dove.

"Certainly not," Veronica replied quickly, surprised at how much his smile could stir her senses. During their many miles of travel he'd seemed to have tamed the wild nature within him where she was concerned, but here now, in his grin, was proof that the same still

lingered. For some absurd reason, this pleased Veronica. "It—it would not be proper," she added, more to her own self than to Julian.

"Precisely. In the event you haven't noted, my lady, may I point out I am doing my best to be a proper employee?"

Oh, she had noticed all right. Since leaving Ripon he'd not once addressed her by her given name and had made great pains not to be alone with her. He'd taken seriously his duties as guard, surveying for himself her rented rooms when they'd taken lodging, standing as sentinel while she dined, and riding ahead of or behind the carriage, ever watchful for any signs of trouble.

"That—that is another thing I wished to speak with you about," Veronica said. "Your change in behavior."

"I thought it would please you."

"Please me? I simply find it suspect. In fact, I think it is one more indication you've something afoot. Tell me," she demanded. "What has Shelton put you up to? Have you perhaps fashioned some sort of bargain with the man?"

"Bargain? Such as what, my lady?"

"Such as," Veronica said, deciding to just be blunt, "going before my father and informing him of all that transpired at Fountains. Doubtless my coachman would delight in placing before the earl a person who could give a firsthand account of my doings."

Julian slanted a glance at her. "To which 'doings' are you referring? When you allowed me to lead you away from your coachman . . . or when I touched you and kissed you—and you returned those kisses with a sweet ardor that would have made even the abbey's white-robed Cistercian monks of old rethink their vows?"

Veronica's cheeks pinked. Oh, yes. That dangerous,

bold, and daring stranger she'd met at Fountains still resided within him.

"Certainly not *that,*" she snapped, looking quickly away. "Besides, you—you'd be a fool to do so. Trust me, my father's reaction should he be informed of the liberties you took would be most unpleasant—for both you *and* me."

Liberties she'd *allowed* to be taken, Veronica reminded herself sharply, feeling the heat of shame suffuse her.

But on the heels of that shame, blast it all, came a whirling surge of excitement washing through her as she remembered, once again and in full detail, the kisses she and Julian had shared at the ruins.

"Then you must, of course," Julian said quietly, cutting into her thoughts, "be referring to your Venus Mission and the package."

Veronica brought her mind back to the present, nodding curtly.

"That is precisely what I am referring to." She looked at him. "Will you be sharing what you know with my father?"

"Do you actually believe I would do that?"

"For a high enough price, I think *any* man would do that," she said.

"Then I do believe, my lady, your opinion of the male species needs altering." He led his mount a tad closer to her own. "Tell me, is there *no* man you trust?"

Julian's attention on her was keen and Veronica had a strong sensation that her answer to his question was very important to him, though she could not fathom why it should be so.

"There—there is one man," she finally admitted, thinking of Sidney, Pamela's youngest brother. Sid would have come with her to Fountains to help retrieve the package if she'd but asked, but he'd had business in Hampshire and had been gone from London for several days. She'd not had the opportunity to wait for him and so had been forced to go the journey alone with just her maid and her judgmental coachman.

"He—he is a very dear friend of mine in Town," she added, thinking fondly of Sid with his angelic face, bright blue eyes, wheat-gold hair, and easy temperament.

"And is he the very one for whom you sought the packet?" Julian demanded, his tone of voice suddenly turning from casually chatty to threatening.

"And if he is?" Veronica challenged, and simply did so because she did not like the change in his accents.

"Then I'd say you are trusting the wrong man. I took a beating at Fountains that would have likely fallen to you had you been the one to find the bundle. By all rights it should have been this *friend* reaching for that bloody thing."

Veronica grimaced, still feeling sick inside at how banged up Julian had gotten that night. She would always feel miserable about what had happened. His face still looked gruesome, his eye just this day reaching what appeared to be the height of its swelling—at least she *hoped* it had reached its ugly apex and would not become any worse.

"You—you know I feel dreadful about what happened, Julian," she said, her voice going soft, "and that I am truly sorry."

"Aye. The question is, are you sorry enough to pay heed when I tell you it is not your coachman or myself whom you should be suspecting?"

Veronica's back straightened at mention of Shelton. She turned her gaze abruptly to the road ahead. "I've never had any reason to trust that man. He is nothing more than the long arm of my father."

"Then trust *me*, Veronica."

She blinked, taken aback by both his suggestion and his use of her given name. Slowly she returned her gaze to his, his words repeating themselves in her brain.

Then trust me.

But she *had*. Did he not realize how much? She'd trusted him at Fountains when she'd taken his hand and allowed him to lead her away from Shelton . . . and she had trusted him even before that—when she'd let him touch her, and kiss her, and make her yearn for things not even she could fully comprehend. He'd made her hungry for the private things a man and a woman could share, for what took place in the marriage bed between a husband and a wife . . . and for what her own parents had never shared in their marriage.

More than that, though, he'd made her yearn for someone to have and to hold and to always turn to, for a safe embrace and a shelter through every storm or sweet sunset life had to offer.

Blast him, did he truly not comprehend how very much she'd already trusted him?

"Your coachman," he continued, "offered me no bargain, Veronica. No matter what you think, we simply came to an understanding, an acceptance of each other, if you will. I tell you true, I'll not be going before your father to tell him about the packet or your mission . . . and I won't be telling him—or anyone else— what you and I shared at Fountains."

Veronica believed him. "Thank you," she murmured, not certain she wouldn't cry.

"But there is still the matter of that Pandora's box of a bundle that has stirred up so much trouble. Even though I'll not be going to your father with any tales or truths, I *will* be living under your roof once we get to London. And I will make it my business to shadow your every step."

Veronica's threat of tears suddenly vanished. He'd done it again. He had made her feel weak-kneed and tenderhearted, then pulled the earth out from under her by becoming overbearing and forceful. "There is no need," she shot back. "No one is even following us."

"How can you be so certain?"

"Because of your vigilance. You—you've seen no signs of anyone. We've had no trouble."

"True. But that doesn't mean those river rats aren't keeping a careful distance. They could be biding their time until we reach London . . . until they see where this carriage finally stops."

Veronica swallowed heavily, but lifted her chin all the same. "Once again you are purposely trying to frighten me."

"Aye. I'd rather *I* did the deed then someone else. If I frighten you enough into being careful, Veronica, you just might live to see this Venus Mission of yours to an end."

"Speaking of which, where *is* the bundle? Do you even have it?"

He patted his saddle with one hand. "Right here," he replied, "and here it will stay until we reach London and you send word to your 'dear friend.' When that person comes for the package, I'll hand it over."

"And then?" she demanded.

"Then, my lady?"

Veronica tamped down the urge the gnash her back teeth together. "Your self-imposed duties as my guard should be finished at such a time, yes?"

"That all depends."

"Depends on what?"

"On whether or not I decide if this 'friend' is worthy of you."

"Somehow, I've the feeling you've already formed your opinion."

He said nothing in reply. Veronica was glad enough for his silence.

They moved along at an easy pace, the carriage following behind.

The sun was bright, and the sound of the horses' hooves and the carriage wheels on the road seemed somehow satisfying to Veronica. Though she dreaded the too-near future of opening the sheepskin bundle with Pamela and what might come of it, and though she wondered if her father had returned from Bath to find her gone, she was, at the moment, enjoying the freedom of the open road and the warmth of the June sunshine.

After a long measure, Julian asked, "Will you tell me a little about your life in London? Since I will be a part of it for however brief or long a time I should know a bit, don't you think?"

"You'll only be involved as much as a guard would be," she reminded him.

"Of course. Only as much as that," he agreed, a shade too easily, she thought.

Veronica was quiet for a moment, trying to decide how much or how little to share. But it seemed the summery day held a magic of its own, one that lulled her into a less cautious frame of mind. "My family resides in Grosvenor Square," she said. "There is my sister, Lily, a year older than myself at one-and-twenty, and our father."

"And too many servants," he added, gazing at her.

"Yes, and too many servants."

"Do you like London?"

"No," she said simply, not even having to think

about her answer. "I do not. I've lived at many of my father's estates. But I spent the bulk of my childhood in Devonshire, and I would have been perfectly content to remain there. But I've vowed to stay in the city until my sister chooses a husband and is safely wed."

" 'Safely wed?' You make it sound as though the road to the altar is a treacherous path."

"For Lily it could be just that." Veronica frowned, deciding she might just as well be totally honest with Julian since he would be hovering near her all the while once they reached London—and the truth of the matter was, he might just prove to be helpful in watching over Lily's welfare as well as her own.

"There is something you should know about my sister. Lady Lily . . . she is not like most other people."

"How do you mean?" Julian asked quietly.

"She—she has a difficult time in learning things, in comprehending. When she was introduced to Society, people thought her charmingly naive—and they still do—but unfortunately it goes much deeper than that. She has the mind of someone younger than her years, and always will."

"So you've always watched over her," he guessed.

Veronica nodded. "My father—he's never shown much interest in his family. My mother, when she was alive, soon lost patience with Lily, glad enough to leave us in the care of some aged governess who had not the slightest idea how to go about teaching my sister. When Lily was very young she needed to be gently coaxed in her learning, to have one repeat and repeat her lessons."

"Which you did."

"Yes. Helping her to learn her letters was a very long process; but as she grew older, and our lessons focused more on social graces, she truly blossomed. As you will soon see for yourself, Julian, my sister is—

she is a very beautiful woman. Given that, and the fact she is the daughter of a very wealthy earl, she does not lack for suitors. Unfortunately, Lily . . . is—is rather in love with the notion of being in love, and while she may not possess a sharp, mental intellect she does harbor a huge and generous heart—one, I am afraid, she tends to give away far too often."

"And her sister?" Julian asked. "Has she, too, perhaps given her heart to someone?"

Veronica glanced at him. " 'Tis a bold question, sir."

"Aye," he acknowledged, making no apology. "Will you answer it?"

Veronica drew in a small breath at how intensely his gaze focused on her, remembering once again the words of Shelton's guide, Drubbs, when he'd claimed that The Riverkeep could look at people and read what was in their souls.

Was Julian doing so now? Could he possibly see in her how much his presence moved her, how his touches and his kisses had branded their stamp upon her soul, forever altering her? Good Lord and good Lord. She felt suddenly naked, her entire being laid bare for him and him alone.

Veronica moistened her suddenly dry lips, saying, "I-I've no interest in finding a husband."

But the words—the very ones she'd said so often to herself, silently—suddenly rang hollow in her ears. She was no longer the same person she'd been when she'd first traveled this road to Ripon and Fountains. She felt, somehow, as if she'd traveled to the stars and back and not simply just north to Yorkshire.

"So there is no special someone in your life, my lady?" Julian asked quietly.

There is you in my life, Veronica thought.

She was amazed at how quickly those words came winging into her brain . . . and amazed even more by the fact she could suddenly not recall just exactly what her life had been before a dangerous stranger lifted her up from the jaws of some wild dogs and then bore her away to safety in that ruinous abbey.

Veronica shook her head, trying to clear her mind of all this man could make her feel and think and do.

"As usual, Julian, our—our conversation has threaded into areas a lady ought not be discussing with—"

"With her personal guard?"

"With *any* man."

"So there is no special other?"

"I didn't say that."

"No. You didn't." He sighed, tipped back the brim of his hat, resettled himself atop his saddle, and said, "Very well. I'll not press."

Was that disappointment etched on his brow? Veronica wondered. Could he perhaps be truly interested in whether or not there was a serious suitor in her life?

But what did it matter? she thought in the next instant, for surely it did not signify. The two of them were from opposite worlds. Clearly something, some horrible happening, had driven Julian to Fountains— either something he'd done, or something that had been done to him.

Whatever it was, he was now going to London with her only because of the beating he'd taken at the hands of those ruffians. Once the mystery of Rathbone's packet was solved, Julian would slip out of her life just as quickly as he'd entered it, returning to God only knew where to do God only knew what. . . .

And Veronica would continue on with her Venus Missions, would watch over Lily until she was safely wed to a man who would marry her for love and love only, and then . . . ?

Ah, then, Veronica would do as she'd always planned to do. She would wait until her next natal day—which was not so far off—when she could claim the inheritance left her by her maternal grandmother, and she would announce to the earl she had no intentions of marrying or of even remaining beneath his roof. Then she would travel, as she'd always longed to do, and she would become an eccentric, independent spinster, but she would not care. She would be alone, but she would not care about that either. After all, it had been the dream of one day claiming her independence that had kept her sane throughout her young adulthood.

But she was fooling herself, Veronica knew. For suddenly, beneath this bright, June sun, that dream—the one she'd always held close—seemed empty, lacking. What had once seemed a grand plan now appeared plain to her to be but a shell of an existence.

Veronica glanced at Julian from beneath the rim of her hat, knowing he was the very one who'd fanned to life in her a spark better left untouched . . . a spark that now needed to be fed by something Veronica had long avoided: *love.*

Twelve

Shelton brought the carriage to a halt in front of the huge, austere manor in Grosvenor Square that was Wrothram House.

Julian dropped down off his saddle, gazing up at the place that, while grand, appeared void of any welcoming warmth or cheeriness.

Just as Shelton moved off his bench to let down the iron rungs and assist Lady Veronica to the pavement, the door of the house opened and a butler emerged.

A tall, thin man with a powdered bagwig and an immutable frown, he hurried forward to stand before the carriage door, ignoring Shelton and giving Julian an up-and-down glance followed by a look of pure disdain.

Julian considered tipping his hat and giving the uppity man a jaunty grin, but thought better of it.

The butler then bowed as Veronica alighted from the carriage. "My lady, welcome home."

"Simms," Veronica acknowledged, glancing over at Julian and then at Wrothram House, clearly nervous now that she'd brought him to her family's home. "Is Earl Wrothram in residence?"

"No, my lady. Still in Bath, he is."

Julian watched as Veronica's slim shoulders relaxed somewhat at that news. "And my sister?" she asked.

Simms's thin-lipped frown increased as he replied,

"Gone with Lady Jersey to visit the ill and infirm, my lady."

Clearly, the ill, the infirm, and Julian could go to the fiery Pit as far as this bewigged butler was concerned. Julian instantly disliked the man, and he wondered how Veronica had managed to endure having such an odious being in her father's employ.

Veronica nodded at Simms, and then, her voice dropping a note lower, said, "I wish for one of the footman to go now to the Beven establishment and send word to Lady Pamela and her brother, the Honorable Sidney Greville, to join me here within the hour, Simms. Will you see that such a message is delivered?"

The butler's thin lips pursed with further disapproval. "But you've only just arrived home, my lady. Are you quite certain—"

"Yes, Simms, I am. Please see to it," Veronica cut in.

"Yes, my lady. Of course."

Simms turned to conduct her inside the house, but Veronica hesitated and said, "I'll be along in a moment, Simms. Do go on ahead and see that my message is sent posthaste."

He paused a moment, as though in the mind to gainsay her, but said at the last, "As you wish, my lady." Casting one last jaundiced look at Julian, he headed into the house.

Veronica appeared relieved to have Simms on his way. She turned her full attention to Julian as a tired Nettie came out of the carriage. At Veronica's dismissive nod, her maid seemed glad enough to scurry inside the imposing mansion on the heels of the butler, but not before sending Julian a smile.

Julian smiled back.

Veronica ignored the exchange. "You should see

your mount to the mews, sir," she said to Julian. "Shelton will show you the way. And now, if you would, please hand over the bundle you found at Fountains."

Julian lifted his brows, adoring the sight of her. "Ah, my lady, just because we've arrived in London does not mean I am going to disappear into the woodwork of this large home of yours. On the contrary, I intend to remain even more by your side."

He watched as she wrinkled that deliciously pert nose of hers. "Do not be absurd," she whispered quickly, for his ears alone. "As I've told you, I've a houseful of servants and will not need to have you dogging my every step."

Julian responded with a casual shrug of his shoulders. "Be that as it may, my lady, I am your personal guard and will take seriously my duties as such. I'll not be cast off to the mews like some stable hand."

Veronica glowered at him. "You *heard* me, Julian," she nearly hissed in a fast whisper. "Now please do as I say and give me no problems. All I want from you at the moment is the package."

Julian leaned slightly toward her. "My lady, isn't that all you've ever wanted from me?" he asked, his voice low and husky, and doubtless affecting her given the slight shiver she so obviously suppressed. Julian grinned to himself knowing in his heart of hearts he did indeed hold some sway over her senses. The knowledge was like a sweet drug in his veins.

Veronica straightened, staring Julian full in the eyes, telling him with that gesture that, although she was not immune to his presence, she was just as surely not about to allow him to take the upper hand with her. "You will, sir, conduct yourself appropriately now that we are in London," she reminded him sharply.

"Yes, my lady, I intend to do just that, *especially* now that we are in London."

She frowned at his cryptic response. "The package, sir."

"So you can open it with your friends present? Could it be that one of them is the very 'friend' for whom you journeyed to Yorkshire?"

"Blast you," she muttered, her beautiful, violet eyes sparking. "I want the sheepskin bundle, Julian."

"And you shall have it. But not yet."

She glared at him, clearly debating whether or not to risk engaging in a full argument with him in front of Wrothram House. Her gaze darted once again to the huge, imposing manor. Simms had come back out on the step, motioning for one of the footman to help with the unloading of the baggage. Seeing the footman heading their way, Veronica returned her attention to Julian. "Very well," she muttered. "I shall give you thirty minutes. That is all. You will see your mount to the mews, and then you will hand the package over to Shelton and instruct him to bring it inside to me. Is that clear, Julian?"

"Clear as those lovely eyes of yours," he replied, knowing he had no intention of doing what she asked.

Veronica, incensed, turned on her heel. Then she headed for the door of the house and said over one shoulder to Shelton as she went, "Show him to the mews, Shelton. And he, uh, has something for you to pass on to me. I shall be in the library in half an hour. Have Simms deliver it to me there."

"Aye, my lady," replied Shelton, not giving her any difficulty as he would have in the past.

Moving to the back of the carriage and climbing up on the hind boot there, Shelton began to undo the straps holding the few pieces of luggage in place, then handed the first of the bags to the footman. When the man was heading for the door, Shelton let a slow whistle through his teeth, saying to Julian, "Not five minutes at Wrothram House and you've managed to anger my lady."

"Aye," agreed Julian, "seems I've a knack for that." He reached to help take down the last of the bags. "Tell me, Shelton, what do you know about this Lady Pamela and her brother, the Honorable Sidney what's-his-name."

"Greville," supplied Shelton. "His name is Greville."

"Greville," muttered Julian, branding the name to his brain and wondering if this Greville character had stolen Veronica's heart—not to mention the Eve Diamond. "Tell me all you know, Shelton."

Shelton shrugged. "Lady P and her brother became fast friends with my lady when she first came to London. Their parents were killed in a carriage accident many years ago. Their eldest brother, Lord Beven, became their guardian, acting as both father and mother to his siblings, raising them and doing a fair job of it. Finally took a wife this past year, and there's word this new bride is anxious for the earl's brothers and sister to make matches of their own and leave Beven House so she can fill it with her own brood. The Honorable Sidney Greville is the youngest brother. Has a flair for managing funds, I've heard. There's a middle son, off studying somewhere. Lady P was betrothed this past spring to some swell—a Lord Rathbone . . . Darius Rathbone—yes, that's the name."

"Rathbone?" Julian repeated, a stirring of feeling flaring to life in his gut and a memory coming alive in his mind.

"Aye," said Shelton, glancing down at Julian. "You know of him?" And then, after a split second of gauging the look on Julian's face, he said, "No, no, don't answer that. I can see that you do, just as I can see you're no lowly riverkeep or even some guard-for-hire.

Far as I can tell, you've got a secret or two, and for whatever reason have come to Wrothram House to keep that secret safe . . . or mayhap reveal someone else's.''

Julian lifted one brow. "You're coming to know me too well, it appears."

"Aye," he said. "Well enough to wager you're knee-deep in something havey-cavey, though not of your own doing, I reckon."

The footman returned then for the remaining bags and both Julian and Shelton fell quiet until he got on his way again.

Once the man was out of earshot, Shelton added, "In fact, I'm coming to know you well enough, Julian, that I've decided, if you be needing any help with what it is you're involved in, you can count on me. I've spent some time in a boxing academy and can hold my own and then some, if you get my meaning."

Julian smiled up at him. "Thank you, Shelton. I might just make good on that offer. In fact," he said, looking once again at the daunting house, "I think I shall begin this moment. Tell me, how do I find your lady's library? I'd like to deliver the, uh, parcel she desires. In person."

Shelton let out another low whistle as he refastened the straps, then climbed down to the ground. "You're a bold one, you are. You'll have to get past that old bag Simms and every dour-faced footman in that house." But then he grinned, clearly relishing the idea of Julian daring to go against the wishes of the haughty butler. "You can enter by the servants' entrance. Come on, I'll tell you the lay of the place, and I'll even see to that fine bit of horseflesh of yours. Earl Wrothram spares nothing for the stabling of his many carriages and cattle in Town. I'll make sure the beast gets a good rubdown and is settled in nice and right."

* * *

Less than thirty minutes later, Julian moved through the cavernous downstairs hall of Wrothram House heading in what he hoped was the general direction of the library. He held the sheepskin bundle in one fist and his worn hat in the other. Just as he reached the large front hall, with its vaulted ceiling, marbled floor, and central curved staircase, he met with the butler.

"Good heavens," Simms breathed, coming to a halt, his thin nostrils pinching together in disgust at sight of the bearded, long-haired Julian inside the house.

"Hullo—Simms, isn't it?" said Julian, casting the man a wide grin. "The name's Julian, sir. I'm to have an audience with your lady in the library. Can't recall it's exact direction, though. Care to lead me there?"

Simms appeared on the verge of apoplexy. "I shall be leading you nowhere but *out*," he said, thoroughly appalled at Julian's presence.

It was at that exact moment that Veronica, having freshened up from her travels, came down the huge staircases, which curved upward to the floor above. She took one look at Julian speaking with her butler and her face went ashen.

"My lady," began the bewigged Simms, his own face scarlet with anger, and his tone barely suppressing his disgust. "I know not what is afoot here, but I insist that this—this *person* be shown the door."

Veronica sent Julian a sharp, reproving glance. To the butler, she said, "That won't be necessary, Simms. You see, I . . . he is—" The sounds of another carriage on the drive outside saved her from continuing. "Ah, that should be Lady Beven and Mr. Greville, Simms.

Do hurry to greet them, and show them into the library."

The butler stiffened, sniffing haughtily. "Such goings on, and with your father gone. He will not be pleased."

"Simms, the door, if you would," Veronica replied, clearly fighting down a shudder of fear at mention of her father.

Julian sobered at the sight of her reaction. He reminded himself that everything he did could land Veronica in a great deal of ugliness with her father. He'd decided miles ago that he very much wanted to meet with this fearsome earl—and *not* as Veronica's hired guard, but as the seventh Earl of Eve, as an equal peer of the realm . . . and as a man who could and would see that Veronica had a day of reckoning with the beastly father she so obviously feared. Julian wanted that very much.

As all of these thoughts went through Julian's mind, Veronica finished descending the stairs and hurried toward him. *"You,"* she whispered hotly as Simms reluctantly went to do her bidding, "come with me."

She navigated him to the left, then down the long hall. Clearly just barely controlling her anger, she thrust open the huge doors to their right and issued him inside the library, which proved to be just as cheerless as the rest of house.

"Have you no concern over what your behavior might bring down upon my ears?" she demanded once they were safely behind closed doors, out of earshot of any of the servants. She paced deep into the room, her hands clenching and unclenching into fists at her sides. "Really, Julian, I'd wanted to deal with your presence in this house in a slow and careful way. But what do I find? *You* standing toe to toe with, of all servants, Simms! Good heavens. Simms has been employed here for all of my father's life and half of his own! Do you not realize what a horrid time I'll have of it when Simms bends my father's ear with how you presented yourself to him?''

Julian allowed Veronica the opportunity to fully chastise him for his bold and stupid way of entering the house. She was correct. He'd bungled things and could only land her into deep waters where her father was concerned, and so, hoping to appease her, he allowed her to ring a peal over his head—which she did magnificently, Julian thought.

As she paced, he watched how the sunlight streaming through the high windows bathed her angry features in a soft glow, how it made her inky locks glisten like dark satin in starlight, and how her violet eyes caught and reflected every nuance of those sunbeams.

She appeared out of place in this forbidding library, which held not a lick of warmth in it, he decided, for she was all that was enchanting and passionate and true. She didn't belong in this monstrous house of ill will. She belonged in a great home built especially for her, one that was filled with light and air . . . with children who looked like her and smelled like her and who carried Julian's fine family name.

It struck Julian then that he'd fallen in love with Veronica. Totally. Absolutely. It had happened the moment he'd viewed her at Fountains, he realized; his fate had been sealed the minute he'd touched his lips to hers.

He wanted to build her that house she so deserved, wanted to fill it with love and laughter, their children and their happiness—a happiness she'd not had in her own childhood. He wanted to construct for her a home very much like the one in which he'd been raised.

In contrast to the memory of Eve House, Wrothram

House was too dark and ill proportioned. The library itself—which should have contained a cozy atmosphere where one to could find respite from a hectic pace to flip through a favored book while sipping a brandy—seemed to Julian to hold the scent of must and unuse, and it had a distinct chill permeating it from every corner.

Julian decided nothing could dispel the coolness, for it seemed to seep out of every floorboard. Though he'd just entered the place and hadn't seen more of it than the servants' entrance and a few halls, the grand dwelling had no warm coziness. It was simply a huge dwelling, with walls and windows, servants and fine furnishings, but no love. It wasn't a *home,* not by far. How difficult it must have been for the beautiful Veronica to move into this mausoleum of dreariness.

At that thought, Julian moved toward her, depositing his hat on a side table near one of the high, wing-backed chairs before the cold hearth as he went. He opened his hand and turned it palm up as he drew nearer to her. "Veronica," he said softly.

"What?" she demanded, furious, pausing only momentarily in her tirade as she whirled to face him. When she saw how close he was, she clamped her mouth shut tight and took a wary step back.

He smiled, loving the spark in her beautiful eyes, the daring in her brave but injured soul, and the lengths she would go for a friend.

"I am sorry—that is what," he said simply. And then, reaching for her hand, he gently unclasped her fist and laid the package atop her palm. "Does this help lessen your anger in any way, Veronica?"

She blew out a small, ragged breath, seemingly struggling against a sudden urge to cry. "Drat you, Julian. You . . . you can be so unexpectedly tender at times. I—" She let forth another small breath, then said, "You continually surprise me."

"Do I? Pity that. What I *want* to do is please you, Veronica."

She blinked, amazed at his confession, confused by it, too. "Julian . . . you—you must cease speaking to me in such a-a familiar way, especially now that we are at Wrothram House. You—you are here as my guard. Do try to remember that."

"Aye," he whispered, tamping down the urge to gather her in his arms and hold her tight. "I shall try, my lady. But there may come a time, I hope, when you see me in a different light."

"Please," she said. "Let us end this conversation. I-I am far too tired to think clearly. And when you stand so close to me, I . . ."

"You what?" Julian prompted softly, moving even closer.

Veronica's spunk returned, her eyes flashing, as she said, "I find you becoming all that is improper again." She took a healthy step away, clutching the bundle tight in her hands as she stared at him.

Julian had expected as much. From what he'd learned from Shelton, Veronica had no reason whatsoever to trust the male species, and from his own behavior with her at Fountains, she'd not been given any other kind of a glimpse into the male mind.

Julian wanted desperately to make amends for how he'd compromised her. What he wanted most of all though was to hold her, kiss her, and make her his own—though not while he was masquerading as a lowly guard, but when he assumed his true role as the seventh Earl of Eve.

There came a jarring knock at the door, and then Simms, at Veronica's call, stepped inside, sending a baleful glance at Julian. "Lady Pamela Beven and the

Honorable Sidney Greville," he announced, ushering the two into the room.

"Pamela! Sid! Thank you for coming so quickly, and on such short notice," Veronica said, moving away from Julian to greet her friends.

Simms lingered in the doorway. "Will you be wanting a tray prepared, my lady?" he asked, his tone indicating just how little he wanted to see about such a matter.

"No, Simms. That will be all, thank you."

"Very well, my lady," he droned, and then, with a final glare at Julian, he retreated, closing the doors behind him.

Julian moved into the shadows of the room and watched as Veronica's friends gathered round her.

The Honorable Sidney Greville was a handsome fellow, with wheat-blond hair and merry eyes. Julian frowned. The gentleman did not seem at all the sort capable of murder and mayhem. Could the package at Fountains have been intended for him? Had Veronica traveled all the way to Fountains for this man?

Gad, it did not seem plausible.

If not that, however, then for *whom* had Veronica spirited off to Yorkshire, risking both her coachman's and her father's ire?

Julian decided to keep mum and find out, his gaze centering solely on Greville. In a stupidly manful frame of mind, Julian decided he could best the young buck blow for blow. For some reason—doubtless because Veronica viewed the man as a friend (and possibly *more* than just a friend)—Julian felt the uncommon urge to punch the man's lights out.

Instead of doing such a thing, however, he schooled his raging thoughts into line and glanced at the man's sister.

Lady Pamela Beven was a petite young woman with

flaxen hair and blue eyes—and the very one, or so Shelton claimed, to be betrothed to Lord Darius Rathbone.

Rathbone.

It was a name Julian had not heard in nearly three years. In fact, the last he'd seen Rathbone had been on the Gold Coast of Africa, many months after the discovery of the huge diamond Julian had dubbed the Eve Diamond.

Rathbone, like many others in the small British trading settlement, had been in awe of the stone. They'd shared some stories around a campfire, and in the morning Rathbone, with his male traveling companion and friend—a Mr. Bartholomew Swann, who had also taken a great interest in the diamond—had embarked on their return journey to England with their huge entourage.

That had been the first and last time Julian had ever seen the man. Could Rathbone have been the one to orchestrate the murder of Julian's family—and all for the Eve Diamond?

Blazes, but such did not seem possible. Rathbone, after all, was not a man in dun territory—or, at least, thought Julian, he hadn't been during that long-ago night in Africa. At that time, Rathbone had been traveling abroad, given to flights of fancy and thinking himself some sort of explorer—though he was but one in the most pampered sense. Julian, being a seasoned traveler abroad, had thought *that* the minute he'd met the man and Swann.

Given that very few people (only his family, actually) had known that Julian was coming to London to help celebrate his father's forty-fifth natal day last August, and that he was bringing the Eve Diamond with him, how could Rathbone have even orchestrated such a scheme to set explosives at his family's Hanover

Square residence, then swiped the chess set—diamond and all—while flames engulfed the place? It made no sense.

Of course, none of what had happened that horrible night made sense, Julian thought now, watching Lady Pamela and her brother sharing warm hugs with Veronica.

"Ronnie," breathed Lady Pamela, stepping out of Veronica's hold. "Is *that* Rathbone's package in your hand?"

Veronica nodded.

"Well? What is *inside*, love. Have you *opened* it?"

Julian watched as Veronica shook her head. "No, of course I haven't, Pam. It wasn't mine to open."

Julian's senses reached a fever height. Here, *at long last*, he'd finally learned for whom that unlucky thing was intended: *Rathbone.*

Veronica, seeming to read his thoughts, finally glanced back at him.

Lady Pamela's and her brother's gazes followed suit.

"Oh, my," breathed Lady Pamela. "Who *is this?*" she asked Veronica.

Julian decided it was time to step back into the light of the room.

"The name is Julian, Lady Beven," he said, sketching a bow. He nodded to her brother. "Sir."

Both Lady Pamela and Greville gaped at Julian, taking in his battered features, travel-stained garb, close-cropped beard, and long hair.

It was Sidney who spoke first. "I say. Gad, Ronnie. What ever did you discover at that wild place called Fountains?"

"A great deal," Veronica murmured, casting Julian a pained expression at her friends' response to him. "Please," she said, turning back to Pamela and Sidney, and motioning toward the desk of the library, with its three wing-backed chairs before it, "have a seat. I've much to tell."

Both nodded and then quickly sat.

Veronica set the fleece-wrapped bundle on the desk before them. "This is indeed the delivery we were after. But I must tell you, Pam, there was trouble in getting the thing."

Sidney scowled. "B'God, if any scoundrel set upon you, Ronnie, I want to know about it. He'll have me to deal with, I swear."

Julian let forth a small grunt of sound. "Ah, if only you had proved so gallant when the lady first set off on her mission, sir."

"Julian, please," Veronica said, trying to cut him off before he began what she could see would be a tirade.

"Please what, Veronica?" Julian demanded. "Absolve him of any guilt he might be feeling at leaving you to go the long road to Yorkshire alone, for the nasty fate that could have befallen you had *you* been the one to reach for that bloody package? *I think not.*"

Julian moved toward Sidney, leaning low over the man's chair and showing fully his ravaged face. *"This,"* he said, indicating his swollen eye and cut lip, "is what awaited Lady Veronica at that abbey."

Lady Pamela gave a startled gasp.

Sidney gripped the arms of the chair he sat upon, his mouth forming a straight white line. "Good heavens," he whispered, then looked at Veronica, his heart in his eyes. "I'd have gone with you on your journey, Ronnie. You know that. All you had to do was but ask."

Veronica, clearly furious that Julian had made such a dramatic display, stepped forward to smile reassuringly at Sidney. "Yes, Sid, I *do* know that, and I bless you for it and—"

"You *bless* him?" Julian thundered, not a little jealous at the way she gazed at the man. He straightened, facing her. *"Bloody hell,* Veronica, you ought to be castigating the man. You ought to be—"

"Julian," Veronica cut in. "That is *enough.*"

Before he knew what she was about, he felt her hands pressing against his shoulders as she pushed him back and down atop the third chair near the desk.

"Sit," she ordered, as though he was but a sheep dog at her heel.

"Devil take it, Veronica. I will have my say about this man and his empty phrases and—"

"And you will hush," she added, her tone brooking no argument. "Really, Julian, this is far and above any crude outburst I expected from you! Now do let me tell this muddled tale."

Veronica, incensed, paced to the side of the desk, leaned her body against it, and began to describe in graphic but brief detail her journey to Fountains and how Julian was set upon by two miscreants.

She finished by adding, "And the men who hurt Julian, Pam, were not after the package, but rather were more interested in *who would retrieve it.*"

"Oh, my," whispered Lady Pamela, casting Julian an apologetic glance. She turned her attention back to Veronica. "All of this *does* bode ill for my intended, just as I'd feared. Oh, dear. Ronnie love, *please* open the bundle . . . l-let us see what is inside."

Veronica surprised them all by shaking her head. "I have been thinking on this, Pam. I believe the best course of action is for you to take this and go before Lord Rathbone. Tell him the truth. Tell him about our foolish mission, but convey to him that it was out of your love and deep concern about his welfare that you even dreamed up the idea of intercepting a delivery meant for him."

"But I couldn't!" she gasped. "He—he would then know I had been stirring into his affairs!"

"Of course he would," said Veronica, "and his re-action to that would be a telling marker as to whether or not he is worthy of your devotion—and *that*, after all, was the entire purpose to this Venus Mission, was it not, Pam?"

"Yes, yes, but still . . ." Lady Pamela's words trailed off, indicating clearly she had no intention of doing such a thing.

Veronica frowned at her friend. "Really, Pam, how you can think to marry a man with whom you cannot be truthful is beyond me."

"I *can* be truthful with him, Ronnie—just . . . just not about this. For goodness' sakes, just look at Mr. Julian and what happened to him when he found the bundle! Darius is doubtless involved in some-thing *awful!*"

"Precisely, Pam, and you need to learn what that something is before you marry the man and make his troubles your own."

"Oh, bother it all, Ronnie, if you won't unwrap the thing, then *I* will!" Lady Pamela quickly reached for the sheepskin bundle, undid the twine, and at the last revealed the black ivory chess piece with its gold base and note tucked inside.

"Return the diamond and chess set?" she said once they'd found and read the note. "What is that? Could it all be some treasured thing in Darius's family, do you think? Is it possible he's being *blackmailed?*"

"Or more likely he is in possession of someone else's property," Sidney muttered after contemplating the note and his sister's question.

"Never say such a thing, Sid!" Lady Pamela cried.

Julian held perfectly still. It took every ounce of his willpower not to react, not to get to his feet and tell

Veronica that he was in fact the seventh Earl of Eve and that the chess piece they all looked upon in shocked curiosity was one he'd helped design . . . that the Eve Diamond had been his final gift to a man he'd loved with all his heart.

But he dared not do any of that. Not yet. Someone had intended to murder him along with his family. To allow Veronica to know his true identity would place her in danger, draw her more fully into the coil of the diamond and the chess set than she already was. And so he kept quiet, though the deed cost him greatly.

"It appears," said Veronica quietly to Pamela, "that Lord Rathbone must possess this diamond and chess set, regardless of who the previous owner may have been . . . and whoever hired those miscreants intends to retrieve it by whatever means possible."

Lady Pamela pulled a small kerchief from her pocket, pressing it against her flushed face. "Oh, Ronnie," she whispered, "I'd not expected *any* of this. Though I'd suspected Darius was involved in something sinister, I-I never thought it might be something of his own making. I cannot believe Rathbone is guilty of—of taking another's property, if *indeed* that is even the case."

"You need to take this to him. Confront him," Veronica said.

"No! I cannot!" Lady Pamela got quickly to her feet. "I am sorry I ever urged you to take on this mission, Ronnie. I want you to destroy everything on this table and—and never whisper a word of this to anyone! I must trust that Darius will—will take care of whatever it is he's involved in and come to no harm." She ripped her gaze to her brother. "I wish to go home now, Sid."

Sidney rose from his chair, as did Julian and Veronica. "Pam, please, only think what you are saying," he implored his sister. "You cannot simply sweep this under the rug. On that table is something intended for Rathbone—a delivery he never received. Surely he will wonder what came of it."

"I don't care, Sid. Do you hear? Darius will deal with it in his own fashion, I am sure—just as he will deal with whatever else he has enmeshed himself in."

"But what of this evening?" Greville demanded. "You are to attend Lord and Lady Mountford's soiree with him. Perhaps tonight you will find the opportunity to ask him about this, to learn what it is he is involved—"

"No!" she exclaimed, horrified at the thought. "I-I won't be going. I shall beg off with a horrid headache, which isn't far from the truth. I *do* feel a headache coming on. Please, Sid, *just take me home."*

She was already heading for the door.

Sidney glanced at Veronica, telling her with a look how sorry he was for everything. "Do you want me to take the chess piece and the note, Ronnie? I'll go to Rathbone myself, though I won't involve you or Pam in the conversation. I'll—"

"That won't be necessary," Julian cut in, surprising both Veronica and Greville, "I'll see to the matter."

"Julian," Veronica said, "we hardly expect—"

"You heard me, my lady," he interrupted her, his tone dark and foreboding, his black gaze centered solely on Greville.

The man wisely took that as his cue to leave. To Veronica, he said, "I shall talk with Pam, then send word to you. Thank you for all of your help, Ronnie."

Veronica sent a warning glance at Julian. Then, with a smile for Greville, she put her arm through the crook of his, saying, "I'll see you out, Sid."

Julian let the lot of them go. Once the door was shut, he sank back down into the chair and stared moodily at the chess piece. It wasn't Greville for whom the piece was intended, but Rathbone. Still, Julian felt little gladness at the discovery. At the moment, he had something else on his mind.

Some moments later, Veronica returned.

"Are you in love with Sidney Greville?" Julian asked bluntly.

Thirteen

Veronica came to a breathless halt just inside the library doors. Julian had leaned back into the cushions of the high wing-backed chair he sat upon, his long legs sprawled out in front of him, his gaze a dark mask as he stared, unseeing, at the sheepskin, chess piece, and note atop the desk.

For the barest of moments Veronica considered passing his question off as being too personal—but in the next instant knew she would be doing no such thing. Her own words to Pam, about being truthful with a man she loved, rang loud in her ears.

And Veronica *did* love Julian. She knew that now; she had known it to be so, perhaps, when he'd first kissed her at the abbey.

Quietly, she moved deeper into the room, not pausing until she reached the side of his chair. "No, Julian," she whispered "I am not in love with Sidney. If you must know, I-I have never loved any man." *Until I met you,* she thought.

Julian glanced up at her, eyes heavy lidded, his darkling gaze burning into hers. "You appeared quite enamored of him . . . and he of you."

"He is my friend. He and Pamela both." Veronica drew in a breath, sighed, then moved to the chair beside him, settling down atop its seat. "Do you remember what I told you about my sister, Julian?"

"Aye. I do."

"When I first came to London I-I had not yet had
my formal introduction to Society. I was not able to
accompany Lily during her many invitations, and my
father only rarely did, choosing instead to allow Lady
Jersey or some other matron to keep a watchful eye
on her. Though Lady Jersey is a dear woman, I fear
she tended to get caught up in her own conversa-
tions and on more than one occasion Lily was led
into some dark garden or onto a terrace by some
less-than-honorable gentlemen." She looked at Julian fully. "If not for Sid and Pamela, I fear my sister
would have been—would have found her reputation
tarnished. I owe them a great deal for helping to
watch over her.

"Though I know Pamela can be flighty and—and
not always prudent in her choices, Julian, she has been
a godsend. That is why I went to Yorkshire on her
behalf. And I am not in love with Sidney. Though he
is kind and sweet, he—he does not stir to life in me
feelings of . . . of excitement, Julian," Veronica whispered, her cheeks heating with a sudden blush, "or
even feelings of desire."

There followed a long moment of silence as Julian's
black gaze devoured her. "And have you ever been
stirred, my lady," he finally asked, so quietly that she
had to strain to hear, "by feelings of excitement . . .
desire?"

Their conversation was threading into dangerous
territory, Veronica knew, but she did not care, for had
that not always been the way of it with the two of them?
Julian had represented himself as a dangerous
stranger when she first encountered him, and from
the moment when she'd allowed him to touch and
kiss her, and later when she'd placed her hand in his
and let him lead her away from her coachman, Veron-

ica had been thrust into a new world—one where she would no longer be ruled by just her brain, but by her heart as well. Julian had opened the floodgates of her heart and now there was no turning back. Only Julian could ask such questions of her . . . and only for Julian would she answer them.

Veronica nodded, her heart beating a rapid tattoo in her breast. "Yes, Julian," she breathed, totally honest now, knowing she could never be anything but honest with this man. "Th-there was one time when I felt such stirring of emotions. Recently, as a matter of fact."

"Oh?" he murmured, gazing deeply into her eyes, so deeply that Veronica felt as though they were becoming one being. "When was that?" he urged, though she guessed he knew the answer.

"At Fountains. And at the inn in Ripon. I felt such feelings then."

Julian leaned forward in his chair, reaching out with one hand and touching the underside of Veronica's chin with the crook of his forefinger. "Ah, my lady," he whispered, "I felt the same. For whatever it is worth to you . . . I felt the same."

He opened his palm, gently sliding his hand back, his fingers softly caressing her jawline, then the shell of her ear. Veronica closed her eyes, pressing her face against his wrist, a soft breath escaping her as he moved his hand to gently caress the side of her neck. Incredible sensations filled her. His hand was rough and warm, just as she remembered it, and though scandalous it was for a lady to be allowing her employee, or any man not her intended, to touch her so intimately, Veronica did not care.

Whatever Julian truly was—guard, riverkeep, or some dangerous stranger who lived life on a sword's edge—Veronica knew deep, deep in her soul that here was a man she could trust . . . with her life, with her heart.

Slowly, she lifted her lashes, not at all surprised to see his face very close to her own. "Julian," she whispered, his name a caress.

He curved his hand against the back of her neck, his fingers smoothing into the upsweep of her hair. "I want to kiss you, Veronica. I wanted to do so that night at the inn, and every mile we travelled back to London."

"Oh, Julian . . ."

"So if my lady has other orders for her guard," he murmured, his gaze smoky with desire, "she'd best give them now."

Veronica smiled tremulously, lifting one hand and gently tracing a trembling finger over his lower lip. "No other orders, Julian," she whispered, moving her finger to the tender cut of his top lip.

He smiled, then lifted his other hand, covering hers and pressing a kiss to the pad of her finger. "You are so soft," he murmured against her forefinger, "so beautiful." He lifted his gaze, drawing her to him with a gentle pressure at the back of her neck.

Veronica let him, her eyes drifting half shut as he whispered a series of soft kisses over her mouth, teasing each corner of her lips, his close-cropped beard feeling wonderfully rough against her skin.

She waited for him to ravish her mouth with a deep, long kiss as he had done at Fountains. She wanted him to do so. Shockingly enough, she wanted to feel him inside her, to have him pull her body to his in a tight, heated embrace. But he did not. Somewhere along the road to London her dangerous stranger had become more civilized, and now he was torturing her with tenderness and feathery kisses that held a hint of the fiery passion she knew to be within him.

"My lovely lady," he murmured, "you deserve so much." He kissed her cheek, the bridge of her nose. "You deserve a fine home of your own—one that complements your beauty and does not threaten to swallow it in darkness as this one. Once I decipher the puzzle of the chess piece and note—"

"No," Veronica whispered, arching her neck as he trailed a path of light, lovely kisses to her jaw line. "I do not wish to speak of Rathbone's package."

"But it is what brought you to me."

"Yes, but—but once the mystery is solved, you . . . you will leave. You will have no reason to watch over me."

"A riverkeep turned guard has no place in your life, Veronica." He lowered his head, dropping a heated kiss to the place where her pulse rapidly beat at the base of her throat.

A shower of tingling sensations coursed along Veronica's spine. With shaking hands she reached for him, threading her fingers through his rich, dark hair, afraid he would draw away from her, would leave her altogether. "Please, no more talk, Julian," she whispered. "I-I am not in the mind to talk just now."

He drew back a little, lifting his face to hers. "There are things you must know about me, Veronica, one truth in particular."

Veronica felt the flutterings of fear beginning in the pit of her stomach. She shook her head, afraid to let him continue. "I-I don't want to know what drove you to Fountains, Julian. Please. I . . . I know that we are from opposing worlds . . . that you are most likely trying to tell me we have no place in each other's lives. But I don't wish to hear that, Julian. I just . . . I want you to kiss me. Now. Please. I vow, if you do not do the deed, do not kiss me now as thoroughly as you did at Fountains, Julian, I shall show you how truly shameless I can be and I shall *kiss you* until your toes curl."

He laughed, a deep, husky sound in the back of his throat. "Ah, Veronica, how I would like that . . . but, my lovely lady, you will hear what I have to say. I—"

The doors of the library were thrust open at that moment.

Veronica let out a tiny gasp, immediately stiffening and pulling quickly away from Julian's touch, fearing that Simms had come to drag him away with the help of the authorities.

But it wasn't Simms flanked by runners who came into the room, but rather the very enchanting Lady Lily, her smile wide at sight of her sister and seemingly filling the room with a waterfall of light.

"Curses," Julian said lowly to Veronica. "We shall continue this conversation later, yes?"

She nodded as Julian got to his feet, easily reaching to offer her a hand and acting as though they'd merely been discussing the weather and had not been on the verge of making love in the library.

Veronica chanced a glance at him, wondering what his initial reaction would be in the face of Lily's supreme beauty. But much to Julian's credit, and to Veronica's vast relief, he did not go slack jawed as every other gentlemen in Town had done. He merely smiled warmly at Lily and sketched a deep bow.

"You've company," said Lily, pausing at the threshold. "Do forgive me for barging in unannounced, Ronnie. I was just so excited to hear you'd returned home that I raced in here like a ninny."

"Hello, Lily. No, do not turn and leave. Come in, come in. There is nothing to forgive, you goose." Veronica turned to Julian to make introductions. "Julian, my sister, Lady Lily. Lily, this is Julian. He, uh, helped escort me home from Yorkshire."

Lily did not find that information at all suspicious or alarming, nor did she cast any judgment whatsoever on Julian, his dress, or the marks of his beating. She was truly delighted to meet him. "Hullo, sir."

"My lady," Julian said, inclining his dark head.

"I vow, sir," Lily replied, "it has been an age and longer since I have seen my sister looking so bright eyed, and even after her long journey home! I suspect your company agrees with her."

Julian smiled, lifting one brow as he glanced at Veronica. "That is my deepest hope," he replied, a softness in his gaze meant solely for Veronica.

Veronica tingled beneath it. She stepped away from him, moving to fully greet her sister. "Give me a hug, you goose. I have missed you so." She held her sister close, giving her a gentle squeeze, then moving back a pace. "You appear rather bright eyed yourself, Lil. I can see you've something to tell me."

"Yes, indeed!" enthused the beautiful Lily.

Veronica laughed, motioning for Lily to have a seat and tell all.

Garbed in a new white day dress, she looked every inch enchanting. Her baby-fine blond hair, so pale as to be almost white, was caught up in a loose bun, several wisps of which had spilled free and now framed her heart-shaped and very pleasing face. She had an aura of gentle, angelic peace about her that not even dreary Wrothram House could dispel.

Veronica watched as her sister, willow wand slim and moving with the grace of a swan, headed toward the chairs. She settled in one, Veronica in the other, and Julian, at Veronica's insistence, sat down in the chair he'd just vacated.

Lily smoothed a strand of hair from her brow, saying, "Actually, Ronnie, there are two bits of news to

share—one is not totally pleasant, and the other is . . .
a secret," she said, sending her sister a dazzling smile.

"A secret?" repeated Veronica, casting a glance at
Julian, and then at the chess piece and note. "Let us
have the other news first, then. Somehow I grow weary
of secrets."

"Oh," said Lily, puzzled, and then, with a shake of
her head, not even considering to press about what
secret her sister could mean, she continued. "The first
news came from Lady Jersey, who heard just this morning from Mr. Heath, who'd been summering in Bath,
just as Papa has been, and, oh," she said all in a tumble
of words, "I'll shall just out with it. Papa is on his way
home, Ronnie. Mr. Heath says he should be here today
or perhaps this evening."

Veronica went perfectly still, dread washing
through her. She had hoped the earl would stay away
for the entire summer, had hoped he might not return
at all—though that last thought was cruel, she knew.
No matter. It was how she felt. She did not wish to face
her father, especially on the heels of her sojourn to
Yorkshire and Simms's grim greeting of Julian. Doubtless the old butler would bend the earl's ear about his
youngest daughter's travels and the man she'd
brought into his house.

Veronica trembled as all of these thoughts tumbled
through her mind. Julian, clearly noticing, reached
out, touched her hand briefly with his own warm,
strong one, and told her, with that simple gesture and
the understanding in his black eyes, that he would
stand beside her if she would but ask when the time
came to greet her father.

Veronica gave him a small, tremulous smile. Then
she turned her attention back to her sister, who was
still speaking, oblivious to the silent communication
between Veronica and Julian.

". . . and so, knowing Papa most likely will not want me out and about on his first evening home, I am hoping you will promise me that we can hurry and be off before he arrives. I do so want to attend Lord and Lady Mountford's soiree this evening—oh, I *must* attend, really, because, dear Ronnie, *that* is when I shall reveal to you my secret!"

Veronica tried to hurry and catch her brain up with what her sister was saying. "Lily, goose, slow down. What secret?"

"I have *met* someone, Ronnie."

"Who? *When?*"Veronica asked, fearing the answers. "Did Sid introduce you, perhaps?"

"No, no, Lady Jersey introduced us, Ronnie. She asked me to dine with her the very day you left for Yorkshire and—oh," she gasped, suddenly embarrassed, "how *was* your journey, Ronnie? How rude of me not to inquire."

"It—it was fine, Lily," Veronica said, looking quickly at Julian, who seemed to take no umbrage at that less-than-apt description. To Lily, she asked, "And this person's name?"

Lily shook her head, smiled, and placed one finger against her own lips. *"That* is my secret—or rather, *part* of the secret. You will meet him this evening, at the soiree. So you see, you *must* say you will come tonight. I know that you must be exhausted from your travels, but, oh, Ronnie, I—I am so very excited about this night. And I *must* have my sister with me. Tonight of all nights."

Veronica did not like the sound of this. She could only imagine whom Lady Jersey thought appropriate to introduce to Lily.

"So we shall go there together, yes?" said Lily, getting to her feet, her blue eyes alight with delight. She leaned down, dropped a kiss to each of Veronica's cheeks, stood, and then, sending one of her thoroughly disarming smiles Julian's way, said, "Well, that is what I dashed in here to say. I shall leave you two alone—though I must say, Simms is prowling about and looking more terrifying than usual. He did brighten at the news of Papa's imminent return, however. It was very nice to have met you, Mr. Julian. I shall be in my chamber, Ronnie, getting ready for this evening. Do come talk with me."

With that, Lily headed out of the library, seeming to float over the floor, so buoyed was she by her "secret."

"Blast," muttered Veronica, standing up. "I do not like the sounds of all of this. It appears I shall have to go to this soiree and meet this 'secret' of Lily's."

Julian had risen, too, and was scooping up the chess piece, note, and sheepskin.

Veronica frowned. "Julian? What are you planning? I can see by the set of your chin that you've got some rig in motion."

"Once and for all I am going to solve the mystery of Rathbone's delivery."

"Julian, *no*. You—you cannot confront Lord Rathbone!"

"Oh? And why not?"

"For one, just look at you! You've the stamp of a ruffian with that swelled eye and cut lip, and *your clothes* . . . you . . . you will never be allowed to get past the man's front steps! Doubtless his servants will summon for the runners at just the sight of you!"

"I believe I know of a way to gain entry," he said, the look on his face dark and foreboding.

Veronica knew an instant fear. "Julian, do not say you would steal your way inside the man's house!"

"I didn't say that, Veronica."

"You didn't *have* to. 'Tis clear to me you've decided

to take a dangerous path, but I-I forbid it! I'll not have you risking imprisonment. Please, Julian. Let Sidney deliver that odious bundle." She watched as he re-wrapped the note, now inside the chess piece, with the sheepskin. Veronica moved directly beside him, her tone nearing hysteria. "Julian, you—you don't have to involve yourself in this mess. You have been too generous with your time already. I could not bear to see you get hurt or—or hauled away by the authorities, not now . . . not that we . . . that I. . . . What I mean to say is . . . Drat, Julian, are you even *listening* to me?"

"Aye, my lady. I am." He finally glanced over at her, surprising Veronica with a heady grin. "I do believe you just said, in too many bloody words, that you care about me."

"Blast you, Julian! Y-yes, I care about you. I . . . I care too much, if you must know the truth, and so I shall not allow you to do anything so idiotic, so perfectly foolish as to go knocking on the door of a powerful peer of the realm—a man, I might add, who could see you clapped in irons for holding that bundle in your hands. Do you think he will *thank* you for appearing at his door with that vile thing? Clearly the man is involved in something sinister and—"

"And as usual, Veronica," he said, cutting her off, "you talk far too much, my darling."

So saying, he silenced her in the only way he knew how. He kissed her—thoroughly, deeply, as he had at Fountains, though this time he did so with every ounce of passion inside of him. His mouth molding over hers, his arms going round her waist, bending her slightly backward. He slid his tongue inside of her, making love to her, seeking out every dreg of sweetness she possessed and plundering it fully, making her his own.

Veronica crumpled beneath his onslaught, her arms snaking around his neck, her fingers working up into his long, soft hair still caught in a queue with the red ribbon. She met his deep kiss with one of her own and held him fast, terrified of letting go for fear he'd leave her, never to return.

He kissed her cheek, then burned a hot path to her ear. "Veronica, my lady, how you move me. . . ."

His breath in her ear sent shivers of delight and desire coursing through her. "Julian," she gasped, twining her fingers together at his neck and drawing his head back with the slight pressure of her thumbs on either side of his jaw. "You must listen to me. Once my father returns home, I-I fear what will happen, wh-what he might do when he learns of my actions during his absence. Simms will no doubt give him a full account of your arrival here and . . . and of the length of time we've spent together in the library."

Julian's eyes darkened. "I cannot wait to meet this father of yours, Veronica."

"No! You—you don't understand, Julian. He . . . he has no great love for me, I fear. He will doubtless take some furious, angry course the minute he arrives. But . . . but no matter what he does, or even where he might pack me off to, I-I want you to know, Julian, that I shall endure it, and I-I will not care because now I know what it is to trust a man and to l—"

"Shh," he murmured, kissing her before she could finish the sentence. "Say no more. I told you, Veronica, I will take care of all things, including Rathbone's bundle and the matter of your father."

She gazed at him deeply, her heart in her eyes. "So you are going to storm all of my castles in just a single day, Julian?"

"Aye, my lady. And then some."

"Julian . . . I-I am afraid for you."

"Trust me, Veronica."

"I do," she whispered. "You know not how very much I do. Before I met you, Julian, I-I never trusted anyone but my own self. I didn't know how truly lonely I was until that day I rode beside you on the way back to Town."

"Which is all the more reason I need to go now. Listen to me, Veronica. I am going to leave word with Shelton that he is to watch over you. No. Do not deny me this," he said when she would protest. "He is no longer the horrid jailor you think him to be. He's sworn to help both me and you. If, when your father arrives, an ugly scene should begin, you are to go to Shelton, do you hear? Will you do that for me?"

Tears gathered in her eyes, and she felt a lump of emotion forming in her throat. "So Shelton has . . . has told you about my past, about my father?"

"He's told me enough," Julian said, and his hold on her tightened protectively. He kissed her one last time.

Veronica clung to him, drinking in the kiss, branding the feel of it, of the man, to her brain. Her fingers caught once again in his hair, and drew the ribbon from the long lengths, her one hand running through the surprisingly soft strands. She wanted desperately to tell him that she loved him, but she knew for some reason he did not want to hear the words—not yet, not here.

Soon, she thought, she would say the words aloud for all the world to hear, and she would not care if the entire Polite World turned its collective back on her for falling in love with a man beneath her own station—because Julian was far and above the lot of them. If not noble by birth, he was so in character.

He broke the contact of their mouths and gazed one last time into her eyes.

"You *will* come back to me, yes?" she whispered. "If not today, then tomorrow, and if not today, you will at least send word to me before the day is out?"

"Aye," he promised. "I will, my lady."

She nodded, drawing in a deep, steadying breath, and then reluctantly stepping out of his embrace. She held his ribbon in her hands, watching as Julian pushed one lone wave of hair from his brow, then sent her a jaunty smile intended to raise her spirits.

"By the bye, Julian," she murmured, telling herself she would not cry, would not become a watering pot in the face of his braveness, "I hate this blasted ribbon. I-I can only imagine how you came by it."

"Then burn it my sweet. Next you see me, God willing, I'll be a changed man, with no need of a ribbon for my hair. I will, Veronica, my lady, my love, be a man who can claim you as his own, one whom you can be proud to know."

"Oh, Julian, what are you talking about? What rubbish is this? You—you are that right now, and more. I—"

"Later, my love," he said, heading for the doors and reaching for the latch. "I shall see you later. I promise. Now do only as Shelton deems is safe. I'll send word to you through him."

"Julian, wait! Where are you going? Will you tell me that much?"

But he was gone, off to complete her Venus Mission . . . and mayhap one of his own.

Fourteen

Julian headed directly to the mews, glad to find Shelton was still there, seeing to the cattle.

The coachman glanced up when Julian entered the stall where he stood smoothing a brush over the shiny coat of Julian's horse. "That bewigged bag of bones boot you out?" Shelton asked. "Though old as original sin, the grim-faced Simms can hold his own on occasion, I'm afraid."

"Never fear, Shelton. It would have taken even more than Wellington's troops to take me out of that house if I wasn't in a mind to leave."

"So I take that to mean you're in that mind, eh?"

Julian nodded, glancing about. "Aye. I've business to attend to. Is there another mount I can take? A fast one?"

Shelton nodded. "I'll see right to it. Anything I can help with?"

"You can watch over Lady Veronica and her sister. I believe they'll be heading to the Mountfords for some sort of gathering. Keep a keen eye, will you? Whoever decided to make a boxing bag of me at Fountains just might come looking for Lady Veronica."

"They'll never reach her, for they'll have to get past me first," Shelton promised.

Julian nodded, knowing he could depend on the man. "Listen to me, Shelton," he said, his tone turning grave, "I am going to pay a visit on a certain deceitful lord. I know not what will come of the meeting . . . or even if I'll be able to hold my fury in check."

Julian took in a deep breath, his hands balling into tight, white-knuckled fists at his sides. "You see, Shelton, my . . . my family was murdered . . . and this man either knows who did the heinous deed . . . or he orchestrated it himself. So after I beat the truth out of him . . . I-I am either going to kill him, or I will be off to take care of the vile fiend who took my family's lives." He blinked once, willing away the emotion storming through him. He had to keep a clear head. *He had to.*

"The reason I am telling you this, Shelton, is because, if I am to become a murderer this night, I-I want you to get Lady Veronica and her sister out of Wrothram House and away from that fiend who is their father. I've a solicitor on Holywell Street. Name is Crandall. You go to him, tell him there'll be a letter of my intentions left at my flat in St. James Place. He knows its direction." He glanced at Shelton, who was now mopping his sweaty brow. "Are you listening, Shelton? It's imperative you get this straight."

"Aye," muttered Shelton, clearly stunned by all he was hearing. "I hear you."

"Good. If anything should happen to me because of my meeting, I-I will leave a written message at my flat. Lady Veronica and Lady Lily will not want for funds should I meet my own demise, or—"

"Be hanged for murder?" Shelton finished.

Julian swallowed thickly. "I've a score to settle, Shelton. And settle it I shall. Now where is that mount?"

Shelton hooked a thumb to a nearby stall.

Julian reached for his own saddle, which had been taken off his horse. Then he headed in that direction, the coachman hurrying in his wake.

"Are you sure this should be the way of it?" Shelton asked, and then growing bold, obviously afraid there was precious little time to be anything but, he added, "I seen the way you watched over my lady . . . and the way she looked at you, Julian. There's love there. 'Tis plain as this once-broken nose on my own ugly mug that the two of you be in love. Why don't you let the authorities take care of this? Better yet, my man, why not let old Shelton here go and shake up that lord? I'll do it, Julian. Just say the words, and I'll make your fight my own. You don't know my history, Julian. I once did that sort of business . . . was paid to be the Grim Reaper visiting in the depths of night. I'll do it again. I'll do it today. You just go back in that house and stay safe. If there's one thing Lady Veronica be needing, 'tis a man like you in her life . . . one who can teach her how to love and to trust."

Julian, having already set to the task of saddling the mount on his own, tightened the girth, grimacing as he did so. Shelton was correct. Julian was risking a great deal in going after Rathbone, intending to beat the truth out of him. Gad, but he was acting no better than the lowly miscreant Veronica had first thought him to be! But he was so consumed with rage right now that he did not dare to pause. If he did, he might never avenge the murder of his family.

Saddle securely in place, he stood upright, and stared at Shelton across the back of the huge horse. "I've got to do this, Shelton. I've waited ten long months. I cannot wait any longer."

He pulled his gloves out of his pack, put them on, then led the beast out of the stalls and outside where he mounted.

Shelton stepped back, knowing there was nothing more he could say to try to stop him. "God go with you, Julian," he said softly.

"Thank you, Shelton. And, please stay near to Lady Veronica. She . . . she means the world to me."

"Aye. And no doubt you've come to mean the same to her." He looked up at Julian. "You never told me your full name, sir. I should like to know . . . if in fact, I'll be having to pay a visit to that Crandall man."

Julian sucked in a deep breath, his nostrils flaring as he looked out at the tiny lane alongside the mews.

" 'Tis Julian Masters, seventh Earl of Eve."

With that, Julian's mouth formed a grim line, he set the beast into motion, and took off, not looking back.

Julian set a fast pace for St. James Place. His flat—housed on the highest floor of a stately building in a quarter known for the untethered gentlemen of the *ton* who kept small apartments there and used them on occasion—was not a grand place. It housed but two rooms: a mezzanine bedchamber, and a main room with a small fireplace blackened with soot.

Julian took the stairs up to the flat two at time, shoved a key he'd retrieved from his saddle into the lock, then burst inside. It was Garn's face he saw first.

"M'lord," said the blond giant, not smiling. "I've been awaiting word from you."

"I came as soon as I could. Gad, Garn, but you must have left Ripon the very night we last spoke to get here so soon."

"Aye. I did. And not alone, m'lord—nor without a certain parcel."

Something in Garn's tone sent warning bells tolling in Julian's head. "*What* parcel? And who came with you?"

Garn stepped aside, waving one brawny arm to encompass the small main room.

Julian's eyes widened at the sight of Garn's son, Wil, sitting atop the threadbare sofa. On the table before Wil, cluttered with papers and maps and such Julian had never bothered to clear away on that night he'd stopped here before traveling to Eve House for his father's natal celebration, was the Eve Diamond, a huge, gorgeous stone, its many facets sparkling in the late afternoon light that filtered down through a musty window in the mezzanine chamber above.

"Dearest God," Julian breathed. He whipped his gaze from the diamond to a sullen, quiet Wil, and then to Garn. "Where did you find this, Garn? What the devil is going on?"

"My son," Garn answered. "It was Wil who had the Eve Diamond, m'lord. Has had it, in fact, since that ugly night August last."

Julian was speechless. He felt as though he'd been given a mighty blow to his solar plexus and could now not even fight to get air into his lungs. *His father's diamond. Here. Not with Rathbone, but here, in this flat, with Wil.*

He moved into the room, fighting down the fury that had no place in the face of a young lad who'd been motherless from the point of his birth and fatherless due to the fact Garn had left England only to serve Julian. He sank down in the antiquated, thickly padded chair opposite Wil and the table with the diamond. Julian folded his still-gloved hands in front of him, steepled his fingers, then leaned forward, pressing that steeple to his tight lips.

He gazed straight into Wil's green eyes, trying to see him for the young man that he was, trying to make some sense of what he'd just learned.

Garn quietly moved to the opposite side of the small room, clearly having decided that his lord would deem the fate of the son he'd claim but had not fathered.

"Start at the beginning, Wil," Julian said, lowly, carefully, trying hard to contain his rage. "How did you come to have that diamond in your possession?"

Wil's face was spotted with two bright circles of red on each of his cheeks—proof he'd been crying, perhaps for a long time. He could not meet Julian's black gaze, did not dare. "I-I had run away from home days before you and my father arrived in London, m'lord," he began, his voice just a hoarse whisper. "I-I'd heard from Aunt Meg that you'd be docking from your—your trip to Africa. I . . . I was sick of living in that cottage, in the country, while my father sailed round the world with you, m'lord. I . . . I wanted more from life. So . . . so I ran away and came here, to London."

Garn ran one thick hand over the back of his own neck, as though he'd known a long, wearying time of getting the truth from his son. "Go on, boy. Get to the heart of the matter. Tell his lordship about the night of the explosion. And the rest. Tell him the rest."

Wil shifted uncomfortably atop the worn cushions, trying to stretch his long legs, but only managing to bang his knees against the table, upsetting the diamond and causing it to rock back and forth and wink its too-bright light. "Very well!" he muttered. "I'll tell it all."

With that, he glanced fully at Julian with all the bold, stupid daring of a fifteen-year-old lad fighting for his independence, and said, "I went to that fine home of your family, m'lord, and—and I waited outside, in the shadows, for you and my father to present yourselves.

"After I saw your entrance, I then peeked inside one of the windows, at all the presents and food laid out in that one room, and I-I just stood there, with my nose pressed tight against the windowpane, wishing, ever wishing, I could be part of a family that was so happy, so filled with love. And when all of you moved out of that room, I stood stock-still, because I didn't want to blink or miss any of the magic of that place.

"And . . . and that's when I saw them . . . saw two men—big, hulking brutes—sneaking around the place, to the very room where you and your family were inside. They bent down near a window, fiddled with something—explosives I-I know that now. Then I-I saw a spark, a flame, and . . . and suddenly it felt like the very world exploded . . . and I-I heard screams and saw the men dash toward me. I ducked, hid, and watched as they broke a window, went into that room with all the gifts and the food and the warmth, and they came out with a wrapped package. I tripped the first man, hit the other in the face with my bare fist . . . and then . . . and then, m'lord, I took the package from the one brute's hands and I-I ran. I just ran because I was so scared and the entire night was just a blaze of flames . . . and the screams, oh, God, they'd gone by then, swallowed up by the sounds of wood burning, and when I . . . when I looked back I-I saw that the whole front of that house was on fire. . . ."

Wil stopped, unable to say more. He jerked his gaze away, staring into the far corner as he wiped the back of one hand across his eyes that were wet with tears. His lower lip was trembling; he was fighting for breath.

Julian sat very still, his fingers still steepled. He did not blink. Did not move. He simply watched the boy, but did not really see him. Instead, he was reliving that horrible, horrible night, hearing again his mother's screams, hearing his sister, Suzanne, only nine years of age, screaming out for Julian to help her because the blast had rocked the very foundations of that side of the house and had brought down a heavy chandelier that had hung in the room, brought it down on top of her legs . . . and Suzanne, dear, sweet Suzanne, had been pinned beneath it, her skirts catching fire, her young body trapped. She hadn't been able to move. . . .

Julian felt his blood roar through his veins as the scene played itself out more fully. He could suddenly taste the smoke in the back of his throat. He felt again as his body had been thrust to one side with the rocking of the blast. He'd hit his head on the heavy statuary his mother had just bought . . . and damn, but he remembered what it had been now . . . a sculpting of a robed Venus! How hideously ironic, Julian thought now.

He'd hit his head so soundly that he'd been knocked out, coming to what must have been a long time later. . . .

Suzanne was no longer screaming. Nobody was.

Flames were all around him. The smoke was so heavy it clung to his lungs and threatened to suffocate him. But he moved, b'God, hearing nothing, but seeing *everything*. His father, the brave earl, flames riding his own back, even his hands on fire, was bent at the waist, reaching past the burning wicks of the chandelier, reaching right through them, toward his young daughter, toward Suzanne, once so lovely, but whose skin had been blackened, her lovely dark hair singed away. . . .

Julian, deaf and numbed by the blast, staggered to his feet, trying to help, trying to save Suzanne, and the earl . . . and his mother—God, his mother!

Julian closed his eyes, willing away the remembered sight. But it was there, as it had always been whenever he closed or opened his eyes.

He saw himself back in that house, that blazing inferno, and he could see his mother, at the opposite end of the room, her entire gown aflame, her arms flailing as she tried to douse the fire at the same time as trying to reach her husband and their daughter.

And that was when it happened . . . when the entire floor above them came crashing down on the far side, just above the countess, raining down on her with flaming wood, spilling down with all the contents of the room above.

Julian cried out, but he did not even hear his own hideous wail. He lunged forward, in one last, desperate attempt to reach his family . . . and then something hard from above came down atop him, and he felt no more, saw no more other then the black wings of darkness fluttering in front of his eyes, claiming him totally. . . .

Julian dropped his fingers from their steeple, pressing them tight over his closed hands. "Dear God," he whispered, racked with remembering, not certain he wouldn't become violently ill. He squeezed his eyes shut even more tightly, forcing himself not to cry, but he couldn't help himself. His family. Gone. From one violent act. Tears streamed past his closed lashes, the bitter salt of them burning his face.

He heard Garn from the opposite side of the room. "Go on, Wil," Garn said lowly, a treacherous note in his voice. "You tell his lordship everything, you hear, boy? *Everything*. This is the murder of his family we are talking about, and you will, dammit, tell him *all*."

Julian forced his eyes open then. He looked at Wil, who sat huddled forward now on the couch, his face in his hands, his young body racked with sobs. Garn, in the far corner, did not fare much better. There were ghosts in his haunted blue eyes—eyes that were usually so merry, but no longer. Clearly, he felt responsible for whatever part his son had played in that fateful, cruel night.

Wil lifted one arm, bent at the elbow, toward his own face, pressing the crook of it to his mouth. He sucked in a deep breath, grimacing as he swiped that same arm across his tear-soaked features.

He finally met Julian's gaze with his own. "After I-I saw what happened, m'lord, after the flames started and I-I hid that package, I ran around to the servants' entrance, found my father, then led him to you. He—he dragged you out of the place, he did. Tried to get your sister, too, and your parents . . . but the house, it just caved right in over them. There—there was no help to be had for them. We . . . we brought you here, 'cause that's what you muttered for us to do. And when my father insisted on getting you to a doctor, you sat straight up, you did, as though you hadn't heard a word he said, and told him to take you to Fountains. Said at Fountains you'd get well. So we—we took you back to Aunt Meg's, and she . . . she saw to what burns you had, and your bruises, and all the while you begged to be left at Fountains, for my father to tell no one you still lived. You swore you'd one day find the murderers. And so that's what my father finally did. Left you at Fountains when you were well enough, so to speak, to be on your own. . . . You—you know the rest from there, m'lord."

"The hell he does," Garn said. "Go on, boy. Keep telling this sordid tale of yours. Tell him about that diamond, lad."

Julian looked from the son to the father, back to the son. Clearly, Garn and Wil had had a long, long talk, and now, the truth would be told. Julian waited.

"I-I thought you went to Fountains to die, m'lord," Wil whispered, shame in his tone. "I never told my father about the package I hid, the very one I went back to claim before we headed home to Yorkshire. When I opened it, and found that diamond"—he nodded toward the table—"inside one of the chess pieces, I knew then what those men were after. I decided to—

to ferret them out. So I ran away once more, back to London, and scoured the worst parts of the city, looking for those men. Found them, too—or, at least, a messenger who could be in contact with them. I-I told them the Eve Diamond was up for sale. Named a high price and told the man to give me his highest bidders. I got two names, m'lord, even a heavy bit of coin from one of them."

Julian finally dropped his hands to his lap, leaning forward. *"Who?"* he demanded. "What are their names, Wil?"

Wil hesitated, and then, pointing to the diamond and to a pouch Julian had overlooked until now, he said, "Lord Darius Rathbone was the first. He paid me in pure gold. It's all in that pouch, m'lord. The second message came from a Mr. Bartholomew Swann. He sent no coin, but a threat. Said I should turn over the very property he'd paid to have taken from your father's house, m'lord. It is Swann who hired those two men to set explosives at Eve House . . . and—and from what I overheard the night you met with my father at Meg's house, it is Swann's men who jumped you, m'lord." Wil fell silent then, thoroughly ashamed of himself.

"You're not done yet with the telling of your tale, boy," Garn muttered. "Tell his lordship the final part."

Wil grimaced. He met Julian's gaze. "Those men were at Fountains to find *me.* Swann had learned that Lord Rathbone never received the chess set and diamond, and he knew Rathbone was sending me word to deliver all of it or else pay the consequences. I'd given Rathbone's messenger—some street urchin—directions to Fountains because I wanted no one to find me at my aunt's cottage." Wil bent his head. "As I told you, m'lord," he whispered, "I thought you went to that ruinous place to die. How was *I* to know you'd finally get to your feet with your hearing, and come upon that street urchin and Rathbone's package? After Rathbone paid me I-I sent him one of the chess pieces wrapped in sheepskin. He sent it all back, I take it."

"That he did, Wil," whispered Julian, finally knowing the full story. "And those thugs nearly beat the life out of me."

Wil winced. "I-I am sorry, m'lord. T-truly, I am." He licked his dry lips, then glanced at his father. "But I did all of this because I only wanted my father to take notice of me. I wanted to uncover the truth of that night, and thought that, if I put word out in the worst parts of the city that this diamond, and the chess set, were up for sale, I'd have the culprits bared."

Julian only nodded, still digesting all that he'd learned. *My God,* he thought, *but I had those vile river rats in my grasp at Fountains—the very same who no doubt laid the explosives that killed my family!* Rage bubbled up once more within him, choking him, gagging him.

He thrust back in his chair, covering his face with his hands. "Damn, damn, *damn them to hell,* " he muttered, his fingers digging into the skin his scalp.

"M'lord."

It was Garn, who had moved to his side. He placed one hand atop Julian's shoulder, squeezed once, and said again, "M'lord?"

"I want to kill them," Julian gasped, his throat constricting with deep, heated rage. "I do, Garn. God help me, but I want to kill those unholy bastards."

"Allow me, m'lord," Garn whispered, his own voice choked with emotion. "For all they have wrought upon you . . . and—and for the part my own son played in all of this, please, m'lord, *allow me.* I will hunt them down, and Rathbone, and Swann, too, and I will see them all brought low and placed in a grave. Let me do this for you, m'lord, and I swear I shall make them suffer as your dear family suffered. Let me do this, m'lord . . . and take the noose as well. And in the end, I'll either see my precious Annie again, or I won't. Whatever comes of it, I'll at least have paid back to you a small portion of what you gave to me by saving me from a life of wandering. Your hiring of me pulled me up by my bootstraps after Annie's death. I'd been brawling my way from one end of the shire to the other, all on a death wish. You ended that life for me, m'lord. And because of you, and your generosity, Wil here has blunt enough to travel the world or to set himself up like a bloody king. He knows that know, m'lord, though but a few days ago he'd merely thought this less-than-fathery figure of his had simply forgotten him."

Julian dropped his hands from his face, Garn's speech leading him back to sanity. "B'God," he whispered, looking Wil straight in the eye. "Had you truly thought your father had forsaken you?"

The young man nodded, then lifted his chin. "Aye, m'lord. I did. What *else* was I to believe? He was gone for years, leaving me to that cottage and those lands and little else. My aunt never told me about all the funds he sent. Never said a word."

"Because they were meant for your future," Garn interrupted. "A future the likes I never dreamed of when I was your age."

Wil twisted a sad, bittersweet smile up at his father. "The only thing I ever really wanted was to have a father," he whispered.

Garn nodded, his weather-beaten face registering his love for the boy not his own but born of the love of his youth. "Aye. I know that now, son.

Julian realized that despite Wil's foolish choices, he

now had two names—Rathbone and Swann—of men who had made a play to possess the Eve diamond and chess set. Both men had been with him on that night on the Gold Coast of Africa, and both men were no doubt as guilty as sin.

Julian looked at the young man. "Dry your eyes, Wil," he said, getting to his feet, "and know I blame you for nothing. Though I took your father away from you, I leave it to the two of you to be deciding whether Garn continues on as my manservant. Between the two of you, you've enough blunt to be answering to no man."

"M'lord," Garn cut in, "I never felt as though I had to answer to you. It was my deepest pleasure to serve you."

"I know that, Garn," Julian said, sending a smile to his friend, who had been with him through so much. "But now is the time for you to reacquaint yourself with your son . . . with Annie's son. No doubt she would be pleased knowing the two of you were making your way together around this world of ours."

"No," Garn insisted. "Not yet, m'lord. Not until I know you've got this mystery of the chess set and diamond solved. The lady you met at Fountains . . . Lady Veronica?"

"Aye," murmured Julian, smiling now as the memory of Veronica's beautiful face floated before his mind's eyes. "That's her name, Garn. And lovely she is. And all things true. In fact, I intend to offer for her hand."

"So she is not connected in any way to the thugs who planted the explosives, who accosted you at the abbey?"

"She is connected, but in a roundabout way. In fact, I shall see her tonight. At a soiree. And I shall go there not as a guard, or a riverkeep, but as the Earl of Eve. Yes. That is what I intend to do, Garn."

"M'lord?" whispered Garn, perplexed. "Does this mean you'll not be paying a visit to Lord Rathbone or Swann?"

"Aye," said Julian, gazing at the Eve Diamond, which winked in the waning sunlight streaming through the high window, "that is exactly what I mean." Julian reached up one hand, running it along his bearded chin. "I think, Garn, I am due for a shave and a haircut, a bath and a change of clothes. Following that," he said, looking at Wil, smiling at the young man who'd made some daring choices but was, in fact, a brave sort who did not deserve to be damned for his role in this sordid story, "I do believe you and Wil and I will pay a visit to the authorities. Wil, my man, are you willing to tell all you know? Giving descriptions and names? Will you help me see to it the authorities have enough evidence to take both Rathbone and Swann in for questioning?"

Wil instantly straightened, amazed he was being given a second chance. "Oh, yes," he breathed. "I am, m'lord."

"Very good," said Julian, thinking of Veronica and the father she loathed, who was hurrying home from Bath to further plague her. "Then I do believe I shall get cleaned up, and with your help, my young man, I will see every runner in this city available descend upon Swann and Rathbone, and Swann's henchmen."

Julian looked at Garn. "My friend," he said, "I thank you for your offer of meeting and dealing with the vile fiends who may be responsible for the deaths of my family. But I must refuse. We shall have the runners dirty their hands and not our own selves. After all, Garn, you've a son eager to see the world . . . and

I—ah, I, Garn—have a lovely lady waiting for me. We should not disappoint them."

Garn's huge face registered a smile. *"M'lord,"* he breathed, "what a fine man you have been to me. It has been my deepest pleasure to serve."

"And now," Julian whispered, sending his manservant a heartfelt smile, "as your Annie would have wanted, you shall see to her son."

"But who will serve you, m'lord?" Garn asked, deep concern in his voice.

"I think I know a perfect candidate," Julian said, thinking of Shelton. "In fact, I think the two of you would get along famously."

"Oh?" replied Garn, perhaps a bit jealous.

"Aye," said Julian, grinning, "though I bet you could box his ears off."

Garn brightened at that prospect. "No doubt I could," he said, sounding typically boastful. He pushed up his shirtsleeves, showing fully his brawny arms. "Let him take one wrong move in serving you, m'lord, and I shall show him up from down."

Julian laughed, feeling better than he had in months. "I will at that, my friend. I will at that." He slapped his hands against his thighs, spearing Wil with a grin as well he rose from his chair. "What say we get a move on, eh, Wil? I am anxious for my shave and change of clothes—and even more so for you to become a man in your own right and go before the authorities with all you know."

"I will, m'lord," promised Wil, getting up as well. "And thank you, m'lord. Thank you for not judging me for what I did."

Julian looked at the boy, with his riotous curls of burnished-gold hair, his green eyes, so clear and filled with both hurt and truth. "How could I ever blame you?" he said. "You have told the truth."

They headed for the door together.

Fifteen

Veronica stood inside the palatial surroundings of Lord and Lady Mountford's home, wondering why on earth she'd agreed to join Lily at this dratted soiree. There was a surprising crush of people given the time of year. Had *no one* summered outside of the city? she wondered.

Sid came toward her, balancing two cool glasses of punch in his hands. "Chin up, Ronnie," he murmured, "the night is nearly over."

"Not near enough," Veronica replied. "And *where*, by the way, is Lily? Drat, Sid, but I left her in your care when I was pulled into some mindless conversation with Lord Mountford. Can that man talk of nothing but the falcons he keeps on his country estate? Gad, but you'd think it was a mark of honor to tame such a bird!"

"It is, Ronnie," Sidney Greville softly reminded her. "As for your sister, I am afraid I left her in the care of one Mr. Bartholomew Swann when she all but begged me to retrieve for her a glass of this too-sweet punch." He held up the two glasses he carried, looking perplexed as to what to do with the second glass after he'd pressed the first into one of Veronica's gloved hands.

"Devil take it, Sid. Just drink it, will you? Gulp it down if you must. *We need to find Lily.*"

"I doubt very much Swann would dare do anything untoward in *this* crush. I say. Ronnie, it's a veritable hothouse in here. Swann could hardly spirit her off to have his way with her."

Veronica frowned. "Really?" she muttered. "I wouldn't wager on that were I you, Sid." She glanced over the sea of faces surrounding them, her eyes narrowing as she spied the aged but still-lovely Lady Jersey. "There is Lady J, Sid. Let us move in her direction and see what we can learn."

"Zounds," he muttered, enduring the tight squeeze to Lady J's side. "I should have stayed home with Pam, begging off with a headache."

Veronica cast him a smile. "But you didn't, Sid, and for that I am grateful. I-I only wish Jul—" She stopped herself from saying more.

"Go on," Sidney pressed. "Say it, Ronnie. Say the words. You only wish your mysterious Mr. Julian had shown his face here tonight."

"Very well," Veronica admitted. "I do wish exactly that."

"Yes, well, fortunate for you he *hasn't!* Zounds, Ronnie, but the man looked an absolute baggage—what with his swollen eye, cut lip, untidy clothes, and his long, shagged hair caught up in that ridiculous ribbon!"

A ribbon, Veronica knew, that she'd tucked into her reticule, unwilling to burn it as Julian had suggested. She had not wished to douse his memory in any way, and she'd waited all the day for some word from him via Shelton.

No word had come, however. And too soon, Veronica found her sister insisting she dress for the soiree, then shooing her out the door of Wrothram House ahead of her. The one and only bright spot of the day had been the fact that their father had not yet arrived home from Bath.

"Mr. Julian is—is not so terrible," Veronica said to Sidney. "In fact, he was . . . was quite chivalrous with me during our long journey home from Yorkshire."

"A beggar, to be sure," Sidney said, appalled. "He is after a healthy purse. Would like nothing better than to put up his heels in your father's fine house."

Veronica glanced sharply at Sidney. If the man could deem Wrothram House a fine one, he surely had no clue how truly miserable it was to reside there, Veronica thought indignantly.

But Julian had guessed such to be true. And right away, at that.

Veronica was glad when they finally reached Lady Jersey's side.

When at last confronted with the question of where the too-beautiful Lily might be, Lady J wrinkled her nose, sniffed haughtily . . . and then, besieged by a guilty conscience, suddenly took Veronica by the elbow and said, "My dearest Veronica, but don't you *know?*"

"Know what?" Veronica asked.

"That your sister is *in love.*"

Veronica had deduced as much. "Lily is ever in love, Lady Jersey. She—"

"No, no," the lady interrupted. "I mean *truly* in love. Why she—she has gone off to Gretna Green with none other than Mr. Bartholomew Swann, and I for one think it a wonderfully romantic notion. Wish I'd done so myself many years ago instead of enduring all the fuss of a huge wedding. They left by the back terrace entrance just a moment ago. She said she'd wanted you to meet her intended, but couldn't get a word in edgewise what with Lord Mountford bending your ear about falcons and such . . . and oh, my, she . . . she just *hurried off.* Said to tell you good-bye and that she'd send word once she'd reached Gretna."

Veronica reacted as though she'd just been touched with a hot, blazing iron. "Blast and damn," she whispered heatedly, surprising Lady Jersey with her unladylike outburst.

"My dear," said Lady J. "I thought you *knew."*

"You thought wrong," said Veronica, her mind calculating how far Lily and Swann could have gotten in this brief span of time.

She swung abruptly away from the lady, nearly knocking Sid over.

"Zounds, Ronnie!" he gasped.

"Zounds indeed, Sid," she said darkly.

There came a commotion from the door to the ballroom just then. Everyone stilled, Veronica included. The many young ladies present drew in silent gasps, the gentlemen, knowing a worthy adversary when they saw one, held their breaths. And the liveried servant, back straight, his head titled high, announced the arrival of Julian Masters, seventh Earl of Eve.

"Good heavens," breathed Sidney beside Veronica. "Is that *him?"*

Veronica, her attention captured by the tall, handsome lord garbed completely in black, the only relief being in the show of snowy linen at his throat and cuffs, shook her head, amazed. Julian's neckcloth was intricately tied, his long locks shorn, his beard shaved away. His battered right eye did not appear so gruesome at the moment, nor did his cut lip with its telltale pink line that would soon become an earnest scar. At the moment, Julian appeared every inch a peer of the realm.

"I-I am not certain, Sid, but I believe it *is* Julian," she said.

"*He* is the mysterious Lord Eve, the very same so many have been trying to find since his family was killed in a violent fire?"

Veronica ripped her gaze to Sidney. "*What?*" she breathed. "What are you saying, Sidney?"

"Zounds, Ronnie, surely you remember hearing of the ugly tale," Greville replied. "Half of Eve House burned to the ground last August on the very night of the sixth Earl of Eve's natal day celebration."

"*No,* I-I don't recall, blast it all. Gad, I was probably so involved in my own misfortunes that I-I glossed over the tragedy. Damn me," she whispered.

"Now, Ronnie dear, don't be saying such a thing. You're correct, y'know, about being so caught up in your own coil as to not take note of some fire in Hanover Square that claimed the lives of an entire family . . . all but the heir apparent, that is."

But Veronica wasn't listening to Sidney's empty reassurances. She had eyes only for Julian—so transformed, but wholly, uniquely his own true self.

How selfish she'd been, she realized. She'd been living in London, but had not even bothered to involve herself with the news of a flaming house on the nearby Hanover Square . . . fire that had taken Julian's family from him.

With a strangled gasp Veronica pulled away from Sidney and Lady Jersey, pushing her way through the throng to Julian.

"Oh, Julian, *my lord,*" she whispered, her heart in her eyes as she gazed up at him. "Why didn't you tell me? Why did you not tell my your true identity . . . about the fire and—"

"Shh," he murmured, holding her back when she would have thrown herself into his arms, bowing to her politely instead. "Do not mar this moment, Veronica, my lady." He lifted his head, nodding to a few people, smiling at some others.

The musicians struck a waltz.

Julian looked into Veronica's eyes. "Will you honor me with this dance, my lady?" he asked.

Her heart turned over. "Oh, my lord, you know I . . . I would honor you with anything," she whispered, her body thrilling when he took her gloved hand in his and led her to middle of the dance floor, then fashioned one strong arm about her waist.

He swept her magnificently into the dance, smiling down at her, pulling her closer by slow degrees. "I have waited a long, long time to hold you like this, my lady, in such a grand ballroom."

Veronica blushed. "I-I had thought you to be nothing more than a lowly riverkeep . . . or worse." But she suddenly wrinkled her nose, hating that she'd said the words. "No, not that," she murmured. "I never, ever, Julian, thought you to be lowly. You . . . you were always ever true, especially when you first met me."

He swept them in a perfect half circle, inclining his head slightly. "Even when I told you that you were my 'hope and need answered?' You were that, my lovely lady. And still are, and will remain so until the day I die, I pray."

"Oh, Julian," Veronica murmured. "I-I waited for you to send word to me this long afternoon and evening, but you did not. I . . . I had feared something horrid happened. That you went to Rathbone—"

"I did not need to," he interrupted, smiling still even as she faltered over a step.

"No?" Veronica murmured.

"No, my lovely lady. I've an eyewitness whom I led to the authorities—one able to implicate not only Lord Rathbone but also another man with the explosion at Eve House."

"Who?" she whispered, moving more comfortably into his embrace, loving the feel of his arm about her.

"A Mr. Bartholomew Swann. That is who."

Veronica stumbled, not certain she wouldn't make a perfect cake of herself. "Ohmigod," she gasped. "Julian! Dear Lord and dear Lord—"

"*What*, my darling?"

"Swann! *He* was Lily's secret. Heavens, but they are even now headed for Gretna Green! I-I had just been about to go after them when you appeared, and well, I-I've clearly lost my head."

"Say no more," Julian replied, dancing her to the side of the room, then taking her hand in his and leading her past the throng of people and out the front doors of the manse.

To Veronica's surprise, Shelton was there, with the Earl of Wrothram's Town carriage. He gave her a bow followed by a heartfelt grin. "My lady," he murmured, "glad I am to see you made amends with his lordship here."

Veronica glanced at Julian. "*He knew?*" she whispered.

"Only after I'd left you in the library and knew I should be going after Rathbone concerning my father's diamond." To Shelton, Julian said, as he lifted Veronica up and into the carriage, "Spring 'em, my man! We've a mission to accomplish! Head for the North Road."

"Aye," said Shelton, doing as he was asked. "But what type of mission, my lord?"

"Saving Lady Lily from being taken to Gretna Green."

"Oh," said Shelton, hunkering down and focusing on his task. "That be reason enough, my lord, to be sure!"

Veronica was thrust back against the squabs, Julian

catching her. "Should I have insisted you stay at the Mountford's, my lady?" he asked.

"No. Never that, Julian, er, *my lord*. I would have followed you anyway."

He grinned. "The name is Julian, my lady," he murmured, just before capturing her mouth with his.

"Aye, my lord Julian," Veronica whispered against his mouth that was now doing the most pleasurable things to hers. "I shall endeavour to remember that."

"See that you do," he growled.

Veronica laid her body back on the squabs, knowing she was his, *had always been his*.

Miles later, Shelton brought their carriage up alongside Swann's. He took his blunderbuss up from the floor, aiming it at the driver. "Pull it over, man, or you'll wish you had."

Swann's driver immediately relented.

Julian, body tight as a bow string as they'd come upon the man's conveyance, quickly jumped to the ground, then closed the distance and yanked open the door. "B'God, Swann, step out here and meet your unlucky fate head on!"

Bartholomew Swann, a quaking mass of limbs in the face of Julian's intensity, climbed down to the road. "It—it was but a lark, Eve. You must understand that!" he cried. "I-I'd met you in Africa, saw that diamond, and I-I wanted it as my own. I never intended for things to turn ugly. I swear! Just wanted to shake you up with a blast, divert your attention, then have my men go inside and get the thing. How I was to know so much could go so wrong?"

"Save your sorry excuses for the hanging judge," Julian muttered. And then, with all the force he could muster, Julian drew his fist back and sent it sailing into Swann's face.

The man crumpled to the road, out cold.

"*Oh!*" Lady Lily cried, finally poking her head out the door.

Veronica watched as Julian looked up at her sister. "I-I am sorry, Lady Lily. Swann is . . . is not the man for you, I fear."

Lily surprised both Veronica and Julian by jumping down out of the carriage, stepping gingerly past Swann's body, and then saying, "How right you are, my good sir. What a *bother* he proved to be! And to think I'd thought to *elope* with him. Ronnie," she called, finally spying her sister, "you and Mr. Julian must never, *ever*, allow me to house such fantasies again. Do you hear?"

Veronica glanced at Julian, her heart in her eyes, and a smile upon her lips. "No, Lily," she said to her beautiful sister. "You can rest assured Julian and I will never let something like this happen again. Now get in this carriage, dear sister of mine, and let us get back to Town."

"With pleasure," agreed Lily, sending Julian one of her bright, disarming smiles.

He grinned, then looked at Veronica. "Once you marry me, my darling, Lily will come live with us, yes? I'll see that she has the proper husband."

Veronica smiled back. "I shall trust her virtue to no one but you, my guard."

Julian laughed, and then, turning serious, dragged Swann upright by the collar. "As for *you,* it is straight to the authorities."

Veronica stood nervously amid the fog-traced gardens of Wrothram House. Her time on the road to Gretna Green with Julian, Lily, and Swann had taken place hours ago. After that, Shelton had deposited her and Lily back at the house. Then he had driven off with Julian and Swann.

What was taking so long? she wondered for the hundredth time. Shelton had returned an hour ago, telling her Julian would meet her in the gardens. That was it. That was all.

She paced a few steps, on edge, then turned and paced back the way she'd come.

From inside the house she heard the sounds of Simms greeting her tyrant of a father. Dear God! The earl had returned home.

Veronica closed her eyes, terrified of what her father would do once he'd learned she'd not only gone to Yorkshire and returned home with a bedraggled guard, but had gone with Lily to a soiree from which Lily had been abducted and taken north to Gretna Green—and by a man who'd had a hand in murdering a family, no less! God, but she hoped *that* bit of information had not gotten out.

Veronica opened her eyes, trembling in the cool, late-night air of the garden. She heard a sound, turned, and then saw Julian come into view by the back way, from the mews.

"My lord," she murmured.

"Julian," he corrected her.

"H-how did it go?" she asked.

He gazed at her deeply, drinking in the sight of her. "Unpleasantly, of course. Swann and his cohorts will be tried. As for Rathbone . . ." He shrugged. "I cannot say. The man has more than a few powerful men in his pocket. My guess is he will walk clean and free of anything."

"Oh, Julian," she murmured. "I-I am so sorry. About your family . . . your loss of hearing . . . and the many months you were forced to live at Fountains, alone, with no one to turn to."

"I am feeling better now, Veronica." He moved forward, closing the distance between them, then capturing her in a tight, heated embrace. "Better because of you, my sweet. You—you taught me how to love again . . . showed me that there is a life for me yet to be lived."

Veronica tipped her face up to his. "I . . . I taught you all of that, Julian?"

"Aye," he murmured.

"Odd," she whispered, pressing her face against his shirtfront, her fingers curling into the fabric of his coat. "I-I'd never known love until I met you, Julian. You presented yourself as some dangerous stranger, courting me, plaguing me . . . and all along you were exactly what I'd needed."

"And what was that, Veronica?"

"A man to love until my dying day and beyond." She pulled back, glancing up at him. "I *do* love you, Julian. I loved you when I thought you were some nefarious miscreant, and later I loved you as my guard."

He held her tightly. "I know," he murmured. He kissed the top of her head, then tipped her face up and kissed her fully on the mouth, his lips slanting over her own, claiming her for all time. "Marry me," he murmured against her mouth. "Marry me and be my countess, the mother of our children, the warm, sweet body in my bed every night and every morning. Oh, Veronica, my sweet, my darling, say you'll be mine for all time. . . ."

"Yes," she whispered, his mouth raking over hers. *"Oh, yes, Julian. Forever yours. Always."*

Veronica's knees weakened beneath his delicious onslaught of kisses, her mouth opening fully. She clung to him, holding tight, knowing, no matter what, they would always be together.

Simms banged open the doors leading to the garden, announcing loudly that her father was now in residence and wished an audience with his daughters.

Veronica stiffened, and then, when Julian deepened another kiss, she sighed, deciding at that moment Simms could go the devil, and she kissed her husband-to-be, not even terrified by her father's arrival.

"My lady," the butler called in imperious tones.

"Later, Simms," Julian growled, turning Veronica about and pressing her deeper into the shadows of the foggy garden.

Veronica smiled against Julian's mouth, knowing he would protect her . . . would *always* protect her, and would always be true.

"My father will be furious, my lord," she murmured.

"You are to call me Julian," he reminded her, pulling her even closer, "and you are to let me deal with this father of yours. Need I remind you I am the seventh Earl of Eve?" he murmured, pausing to produce from one pocket the Eve Diamond. He pressed it against Veronica's throat. "I shall fasten a chain of the finest links for you to wear this about your neck."

"No. Julian. It—it was a gift for your father."

He brushed away her worries. "And my father shall look down from his place in heaven and see that my beautiful wife wears it now. He will be pleased. Know that, Veronica, my lady, my darling. And we shall pass this diamond along to our firstborn . . . and he—or she—will carry with them our love as well as the love of my father, mother, and dear sister. It will be so, Veronica. Say it will."

Veronica nodded, her heart overflowing. "It will, Julian, my lord, my love. *It will be just as you say.*"

And she knew that what she said was the truth. At long last, Veronica had found true love.